SUSAN'S HELPING HAND

SUSAN'S
HELPING HAND

by

JANE SHAW

THE CHILDREN'S PRESS
LONDON AND GLASGOW

PRINTED IN GREAT BRITAIN

CONTENTS

PROLOGUE

WHEN ANNABEL'S father and mother were killed
by terrorists in Kenya, the only bright gleam in
the gloom of Annabel's future was the thought of
Aunt Evelyn. Her mother had told her such a lot
about Aunt Evelyn, who was so pretty and so gay;
and now Annabel and the two younger ones, Mary
and Robert, were to go back to England to live
with Aunt Evelyn, who had come back from
America specially. For although Aunt Evelyn had
quarrelled with Annabel's parents, or at least with
her father, now she was to be the children's
guardian and look after them. Annabel's mother
had sighed and grieved over the quarrel, and tried
to excuse and explain both sides to the children,
and eventually it had never been spoken of, but
Annabel had never forgotten it. It was all about
a party dress, it seemed, a party dress for Annabel
which Aunt Evelyn had sent. Annabel's father had
flown into a rage and said that he wasn't accepting
charity from anyone—what he couldn't afford to
buy for the children, the children could do without, and the dress had to be sent back immediately.
Annabel had been sorry about this, because one
of the things that he couldn't afford was a party
frock; she had never had a proper party frock—
and this one was so pretty—pale pink organdie
with frills. Her mother had made her a frock of

spotted muslin, which was very nice, but it wasn't pink organdie, and Annabel had always felt that anyone who could have chosen a pink organdie frock with frills must be a very nice sort of person. But Aunt Evelyn's letters had ceased from that time, and so had her exciting parcels.

So that when the children came back to London and met Aunt Evelyn, it was a great shock to Annabel to find that she wasn't as nice as she expected. She was all *right*—she was pretty, in a washed-out way, and she laughed and smiled a lot while they were still at the lawyer's. But she took them to live in a dingy boarding-house in Bloomsbury and from that minute she became less and less nice. It was November, it was wet and cold and foggy, the dingy boarding-house had dark gloomy paint and nasty smells. The children had come straight from the sunshine and bright clean skies of Africa; they pined in the damp dark smutty air of Bloomsbury. But Annabel said nothing. Aunt Evelyn *couldn't* do anything wrong —they were only staying at that horrible place until Aunt Evelyn had fixed something better. Besides, there might not be enough money for anything better. Annabel knew quite a lot about not having enough money and having to make do— still, she had hoped that there would be enough money to buy the children—and herself of course —decent winter overcoats, for their African clothes weren't nearly warm enough. Annabel hadn't an idea how much money there was, but there was her mother's money, she imagined—and Aunt Evelyn must have some because she had wonderful clothes and a fur coat. Of course Aunt Evelyn couldn't be expected to spend her money on Annabel and the children, but how she could *bear* that boarding-house, even if she *was* out most of the day! The children didn't go out—they were too cold to go out and besides, there was nowhere to go. Annabel had asked once if there wasn't a park where they could go and the little drab maid in the boarding-house told her that there was Regent's Park which was ever so nice and told her how to get there. But the expedition hadn't been a success, because the younger ones were terrified of the London traffic—Annabel was too, as a matter of fact, but she wasn't going to admit it because she was almost sixteen—and they hated Regent's Park when they reached it because there were no flowers and Mary said she could hear wild animals roaring in the distance. Annabel said rather crossly— because it had been quite an effort getting them there—that they ought to make the best of it because it was a lot nicer than that dreary street where they lived and that anyway there were no flowers in England in November. And there were no wild animals either so they *couldn't* have heard them roaring. But at these harsh words Mary, who was cold and hungry and very unhappy, burst into tears and Robert turned on Annabel for upsetting his sister and Annabel was terribly ashamed of the whole scene, and the party trailed disconsolately back to the dingy boarding-house. It didn't make matters any better when Annabel found out later that there was a zoo in Regent's Park and Mary had been right all the time.

This unhappy excursion gave Annabel courage to tackle Aunt Evelyn about clothes and schools and living somewhere a bit nicer, and Aunt Evelyn got very huffy and said that she was doing her best and that grumbling like this was a fine way to repay her for all the trouble she was taking over three ungrateful children—Annabel could be quite sure that when she had time she was going to see about some clothes, although Annabel should be the last one to expect a lot of expensive clothes.

"I don't *want* a lot of expensive clothes, Aunt Evelyn," said Annabel desperately, "but Mary complains of the cold."

"Well," said Aunt Evelyn, "Mary is just a teeny bit inclined to whine, isn't she? But we'll soon get her hardy and jolly like English children."

Annabel had nothing to say to this. "And what about schools?" she said at length.

"Well Annabel," said Aunt Evelyn, "there isn't very much money, you know, so I thought that Mary and Robert could go to the elementary school round the corner. And as you'll be sixteen in January, you needn't go back to school at all. We'll find you a nice job somewhere. In a shop. Or an office."

Annabel was aghast. "But—but—Aunt Evelyn," she stammered. "I *must* go back to school and get my matric—I don't know what they call it in English schools. I want to go to the university and be a doctor!"

"But Annabel, darling, beggars can't be choosers you know," said Aunt Evelyn.

Annabel cried herself to sleep that night.

But next day she left the children in charge of the drab little maid and went and saw Mr. Buckingham the lawyer. For weeks afterwards she felt sick when she thought of that interview, for Aunt Evelyn, summoned by Mr. Buckingham, denied every word, and in her soft smooth way made out that Annabel was telling a parcel of lies. She had an answer for everything—well, of course she was going to buy the children warm clothes, but having been in America so long she was quite out of touch with the London shops and had been looking round to see where the best value was to be had. Mr. Buckingham, she was sure, would appreciate that she didn't want to squander the children's money. (And it *is* our money! thought Annabel. All those thousands! For Mr. Buckingham had told her that there was not only her mother's money, but a very considerable fortune left by a great-aunt which had come to them.) As for schools—well, Mr. Buckingham knew, even if dear Annabel didn't, how impossible it was these days to get children into good schools unless their names had been entered practically when they were born; she had been spending weeks and weeks looking at schools in different parts of the country, and at this she cast a softly reproachful look at Annabel.

By this time Annabel felt so helpless and angry that she became truculent, which didn't advance her cause with the lawyer, a dry little man who obviously believed every word that Aunt Evelyn said.

"If we're so wealthy, do we *have* to live in that horrible boarding-house?" she demanded rudely.

"Oh darling," said Aunt Evelyn, "I *know* London must seem terribly, terribly drab to you after the African sunshine, but believe me, I shall be getting out of London just as soon as ever I can. You can't just rush out and buy a house like a packet of pins you know——"

"My dear young lady," Mr. Buckingham said very coldly to Annabel, "I think that we can trust Miss Gardiner to see to everything that is needful for you. And it is up to you to try to settle down in this country just as quickly as ever you can."

Raging inwardly, Annabel went back to Bloomsbury with a still gently reproachful Aunt Evelyn.

But good did come of the unfortunate interview after all, because Aunt Evelyn did buy them coats and woollen vests. The coats weren't very nice, as a matter of fact, which seemed a pity after all the care that Aunt Evelyn had apparently put into the choosing of them, but the vests were all right, and Mary didn't look so blue and pinched and just on the point of catching pneumonia, which was a great relief to Annabel.

The other good thing that came out of the interview was that Annabel knew once and for all that Aunt Evelyn wasn't to be trusted. She could be as sweet and simpering and gentle as she liked, Annabel thought, she wasn't ever again going to trust her as far as she could throw her. "I hate her. I *hate* her!" thought Annabel. "She's sly and two-faced and horrible. No wonder father quarrelled with her. And she hates us. You can tell by the very way she looks at Mary and Robert that she hates children. But if she hates us all like this why did she bother about us at all? She wasn't forced to have us to live with her. And I don't care what she says, she could have got us into *some* school when there's all that money——"

A few days after this, the drab little maid, who had taken a fancy to Annabel, gave her a two-day old *Times* which she had cleared out of the room of one of the boarders.

"Oh thank you, Shirley," said Annabel, thankfully turning away from the dispiriting view of the street, where a mizzling rain was falling. She sat on the floor and crouched as near as she could to the tiny electric fire which, she was sure, really only succeeded in making the room colder; Mary and Robert were playing Happy Families—rather inappropriately, Annabel couldn't help feeling; Aunt Evelyn had gone out—as she always did. Annabel had nothing to read and nothing to do, and she read that old *Times* from the first word in the first column to the last word in the last column—she read the financial pages and the sporting news, the lost-and-found and the legal notices; she read the properties to let and to be sold columns. And while she was reading these one little modest notice seemed to rise out of the page and demand her attention. It said:

KENT. To let furnished. Charming old-world cottage. 1 reception. 2 bedrooms. Kitchen and bath. Main water and elec. Very moderate rent.

Annabel read it and re-read it; went away to another part of the paper and then came back to it. Finally she tore it out and put it carefully away in her empty purse. . . .

CHAPTER ONE

CHICKEN-POX

SUSAN LYLE, while her parents were in Africa, was making her home with her cousins the Carmichaels. There were three Carmichaels—Charlotte who was sixteen; Midge who was fourteen and a few months older than Susan; and Bill who was eleven. Susan went to boarding-school with Charlotte and Midge and spent the holidays with them in their big, beautiful, but rather shabby eighteenth-century house in Wichwood Village, which really was a nice little village although at the same time it was a suburb of London. The Carmichaels had no mother; Aunt Lucy looked after them and their father, who was a doctor and practically always run off his feet.

It annoyed Susan very much that on the very first morning of the Easter holidays she should waken up feeling peculiar.

"Oh dear," she thought, as soon as she opened her eyes. "I don't feel a bit like getting up. I wish Aunt Lucy would let us have a long lie——" This was such an unusual feeling for her that she lay and wondered about it for a little. She sat up and lazily poked her finger at Chang, her Siamese cat who was lying on her feet. Her head felt funny so she lay down again. In the other bed in the big pleasant room Midge was still an

inert mass under the blankets. Midge was always
like that in the morning—it didn't seem to matter
whether she was wakened at six or nine, she never
wanted to get up. But Susan was usually quite
bouncing in the morning, although naturally the
later it was the more bouncing and ready to get
up. She looked at her watch and to her surprise
it was already a quarter-past eight. Bill hammered
on the door a second time and Susan called, "Yes,
all right! We're getting up," and began reluctantly
to drag herself out of bed. She crawled over to
the gas fire and lit it; huddled there for a little
and then began on the task of rousing Midge.
This she accomplished in time, but Midge showed
not the slightest inclination to get up. She just
lay there, groaning.

"Susie, I can't get up," she said.

"But you must," said Susan. "Besides, it's the
first day of the holidays and there are such heaps
of things to do—see how the garden's getting on,
go down the village, take Chang for a walk—
and the sticky buds are out on the big chestnut,
I can see them from here—at least I could if I
stood up."

Midge moaned at the very idea of all this
activity. "I feel so *ill*," she said.

"I don't feel any too grand myself," said Susan,
still huddling over the fire.

"And what's more," said Midge, "I'm itchy."

Susan tottered over to her cousin's bed. "Let's
have a look at your chest," she said.

"Look at your own chest," said Midge, "and
leave me in peace."

Susan unbuttoned her pyjamas and gave a shriek. "Midge!" she said, "I'm covered in horrible blisters! Let's have a look at you——!"

Midge grudgingly undid one button. "Yes, look at you," said Susan, "you've got them too! Midge, what's the matter with us?"

"The Black Death, I should think," said Midge. Susan shrieked again.

Charlotte came in then. "Aren't you two ever going to get ready?" she said.

Midge waited until Charlotte was well into the room and then she said, "Charlotte, I think you should tell Aunt Lucy that Susie and I are covered with spots."

Charlotte looked aghast, clapped her hand over her mouth and ran from the room.

Midge lay back on her pillow smiling maliciously. "And that's the girl," she said, "that's the girl you wanted to make a nurse."

"*I* didn't want to make her a nurse," said Susan. "*She* wanted to be a nurse and I just wanted to help her."

"Yes well, you know what happens when you start helping," said Midge.

"You needn't worry," said Susan. "I've turned over a new leaf. I'm minding my own business. And anyone can die on their feet or break their hearts before I'll lend them a helping hand." She was silent for a minute and then added, "We must do something to help Charlotte with this new idea of hers, although I must say it sounds quite potty to me. I don't see how she can make a career out of collecting broken tea-cups and things."

Midge cautiously rubbed her back up and down on the pillow to try to get rid of the itch. "This is only a craze, not a career. And it's not broken tea-cups, you clot, it's old china. She copied the idea off Anne Hunter who's definitely mental. And her pal Avril at school told me that she was a perfect bore now—every time they went into the town she did nothing but hang around the antique shops and the old china shops and she talks of nothing but Chelsea and Derby and Worcester——"

Susan looked vacant.

"Those are all names of different factories that made china in the eighteenth century," Midge kindly explained to her ignorant cousin.

"Mother's got a tea-set that belonged to her great-grandmother," said Susan, not to be out-done. "It's very pretty. But what on earth would Charlotte do with a whole lot of tea-sets?"

"You needn't worry," said Midge. "Old china that people collect is terribly expensive—Charlotte can't afford to buy one saucer, far less a tea-set."

"Ugh, but I'd like her to have a wee saucer," said Susan. "How horrid to be a collector and not collect a single thing. I *do* think it's pathetic."

"I don't know about pathetic," said Midge, "I do know it'll be a terrible bore. Charlotte's very like Aunt Lucy, you know—they both get the maddest crazes. And now we'll hear nothing but ' hard-paste porcelain ' and ' soft-paste ' and ' biscuit '——"

"You seem to know all about it," said Susan.

"All that rot was in a book about china that Charlotte lent me when I had absolutely nothing to read," said Midge. "That was as far as I got before it sent me to sleep."

Aunt Lucy bustled in and took one look at their spots. "Chicken-pox," she said, and there was general lamentation. "Well, there it is," said Aunt Lucy finally, "holidays or no holidays there's nothing we can do about it. It might have been worse. Get back into bed, Susan, I expect Uncle Charles will keep you in bed for a few days— certainly as long as you're running temperatures. Bill and Charlotte have had it, thank goodness, I'll go and relieve her mind. She's practically bathing in disinfectant and rinsing out her mouth and gargling and changing her clothes!"

"Silly chump," said Midge. "She'll feel an ass when she hears it's only chicken-pox."

Aunt Lucy went out and Susan stared at Midge from her bed, her dark eyes wide and anxious. "Only chicken-pox!" she said. "People die! And their faces get pock-marked and they're scarred for life!"

"*Chicken*-pox, you ass, not smallpox," said Midge, and Susan fell back on her pillows, giggling weakly with relief.

Uncle Charles confirmed Aunt Lucy's diagnosis, commiserated with the two girls going down with an infectious disease on the very first day of the holidays, and promised to give them some stuff that he had had sent as a sample to dab on their itchy spots. "And at least it's some consolation that Charlotte and Bill have had it," he said. "We don't need to segregate them. But it's hard lines on you two."

Well, it may only have been chicken-pox, but a few extremely uncomfortable and miserable days set in for Midge and Susan. Susan, in her usual dramatic way, ran a high temperature and was quite ill. Midge wasn't so bad, but felt quite bad enough ; and for a day or two their only con- solation was comparing temperatures and their respective quantities of spots. In between his own pursuits, Bill entertained them as best he could, brought them books and played draughts and dominoes and canasta and halma with them. Charlotte wouldn't come near them at first because, she insisted, she had heard of millions of people who had had chicken-pox twice, if not three times; but eventually she was persuaded that perhaps that wasn't likely and came and read them interesting bits about the history of china and porcelain which sent them both comfortably to sleep.

One day when the temperatures had subsided and the spots were taking their course, Aunt Lucy was bemoaning the girls' spoilt holiday. "Now that you're up, I wonder if Cousin Barbara would have you?" she said. "There are no children there and you would be getting some fresh air."

The family thought that this was a wonderful idea, and begged Aunt Lucy to go and telephone Cousin Barbara immediately.

Cousin Barbara, who was really the cousin of Aunt Lucy and Uncle Charles and Susan's mother, was a widow and had a small fruit farm in Kent, near a village called Paddocks. The Carmichaels had often stayed with her, but Susan, whose home was in Glasgow, never had. "I do hope she'll have us," said Midge, "you'd love Apple-tree Farm, Susie—the house is hundreds of years old, all beams and little twisty rooms and there's a nice garden and a wood with primroses and lilies and violets and daffodils, and Cousin Barbara has hens and cows as well as the fruit trees and gives you wonderful food——"

It was all fixed up—Cousin Barbara would have the whole family. But she would have no domestic help because her young "help" had a small brother and sister at home who hadn't had chicken-pox and Cousin Barbara wouldn't let her come to the house until the girls were out of quarantine so the family would need to be useful, and they all promised that they would and Bill said that he would milk the cows. Aunt Lucy was persuaded to go too, and leave Mrs. Taylor, the daily help, to look after Uncle Charles who said that he couldn't leave his patients although he might manage down for a day or two at Easter. Susan worried a little about the best thing to do with Chang, but it was eventually decided that he would be happier at home with Uncle Charles and Mrs. Taylor, especially as Cousin Barbara had a golden retriever puppy, although it was said to have a very mild and pleasant disposition.

So they all packed into the car, which was a tight fit and rather uncomfortable but improved when Bill eventually consented to unpack his beloved electric train which wouldn't be much good to him anyway at Apple-tree Farm because there was no electricity in the house; and Uncle Charles motored them to Paddocks.

Susan had never been into that part of Kent before, and was intrigued by the hop-gardens which looked a little peculiar to her as there were no hops yet, only the great poles and strings up which the hops would eventually climb. She liked the oasthouses, which were where the hops would be dried, with their white conical tops like witches' hats, and she liked the pretty villages through which they passed. As for Apple-tree Farm, she fell in love with it straight away, with its old rosy brick gables set amidst lilac and laburnum trees, an ancient quince leaning against the oast-house, old weatherboard barns and outbuildings huddling cosily behind, and the orchards making a bright frame round it all.

Inside it was just as nice, with rambling beamed rooms and steps up and down where you didn't expect them and a fireplace in the sitting-room where you could easily roast an ox if you happened to have an ox to roast. There were two staircases —a fairly ordinary one that led up from the front door (which hardly anyone ever used, preferring the side door from the yard where the pump was) and a steep wooden one, more like a ladder, that led up from the scullery beside the big low kitchen to a neat little bedroom with twisted beams which was to be Bill's—he felt very proud of having his own stair.

"Oh, but we've got to use it too," objected Midge.

"Well you may use it," said Bill kindly, "but it's my stair."

From Bill's room a narrow little passage squeezed its way to the front part of the house and Cousin Barbara's room and two other bedrooms which were also beamed and low and had very interesting uneven floors and the squint windows that Susan admired so much, and old maps of Kent framed on the walls. Aunt Lucy was installed in one and the girls were making for the other when Susan got another surprise. Cousin Barbara opened the door of what Susan thought was a cupboard and revealed another little wooden stair! Half-way up it divided, and one stair led to a little beamed room overlooking the garden for Charlotte, while the other led to a delightful attic, with two beds and a frilled dressing-table and fresh crisp muslin curtains fluttering at the window, which was quite enough out of the straight even for Susan. Her happiness was complete. She stuck her head out of the window and looked out over the cobbled yard to the duck-pond fringed with daffodils, and the old stable which looked like a twinkling old man with funny half-rounded windows for eyebrows and the door for a mouth and an old lantern for a nose.

"'Mm, 'mm," she sniffed. "Doesn't the air smell heavenly and fresh?"

Midge pushed her aside and sniffed appreciatively in her turn. "I can smell wallflowers," she said.

Susan unpacked their things and put them neatly away in the drawers and little hanging wardrobe, while Midge went on leaning her elbows on the sill and sniffing. "Cousin Barbara will love you," she said, casting an idle glance at the busy Susan. "She's madly energetic—always busy and never still a minute. I sometimes wonder what she thinks of us——"

Susan wondered too because on the whole the Carmichaels were an indolent lot, with the possible exception of Bill; although both Midge and Charlotte could devote plenty of energy to things that they called really interesting. Unpacking and tidying drawers and helping with the housework didn't come into this category; in fact, according to Charlotte, it was confined in Midge's case to sitting with her feet up reading a book. Aunt Lucy and Uncle Charles were different too, of course, because Uncle Charles worked all the time, day *and* night it seemed to his family; while whatever Aunt Lucy's natural inclination to idleness she had no opportunity to indulge it for she had to be constantly on the bustle.

The countryside was looking beautiful. Although Easter was late that year the weather had been cold and the season was late too: when Susan and the Carmichaels went to Apple-tree Farm the plum and cherry blossom was beginning to come out in the orchards—the apple trees scarcely showing their pink buds. For the first week the children stayed about the farm and the orchards while Susan and Midge were still in quarantine. There were some baby goslings which demanded a lot of attention. The children had watched them actually hatching out of the eggs in the incubator, and then they had been promoted to their own little house on the lawn with a nice grass run now that the days were warmer—little fluffy creatures, some yellow, some a sort of fawny-green. They needed a great many meals of bread and milk, and to be kept in the sun and prevented from getting wet and helped to their big feet if they fell over and guarded from the too-boisterous overtures of Wendy, the golden retriever puppy.

Bill wasn't exactly allowed to milk the cows, but he was allowed to finish them off and quite fancied himself as a cowman and murmured soothingly to Strawberry, the little Jersey cow and to April, her new calf. Susan longed to milk too, and was allowed to try, but Strawberry and she didn't hit it off too well, and after Strawberry had kicked the stool and the milk-pail and finally Susan herself, Cousin Barbara decided that Susan wasn't destined to be a milkmaid, and she had to content herself with helping to feed the hens and the geese and the ducks, and gathering the eggs, which was a job she liked, although she did show signs of wanting to organise the hens and grumbled every day about one big brown one who insisted on laying under the hedge instead of in the nest provided in the hen-house.

"Oh, leave the poor hen in peace," said Midge.

"Anyway, I rather like getting the eggs out of the hedge—she's made herself a nest, poor old thing."

"She'd be much more comfortable in the hen-house," said Susan firmly. "It's for her own good." The hen, however, continued to lay under the hedge and, according to Susan, always gave Susan a nasty look out of her beady eye when they happened to meet.

They went primrosing in the woods at the bottom of the orchard, and sent cigarette boxes full of primroses arranged on a bed of damp moss to all their friends. Bill became fanatically interested in the routine of the fruit-growing and followed the foreman and the farm boys about, asking questions. Charlotte heard him muttering to himself, "At green bud, at pink bud, at blossom-fall," with a rather wild look in his eye.

"What's the matter, Bill?" she said uneasily. "It couldn't be that you've taken to making up poetry in your old age, could it?"

"No, it couldn't," said Bill, affronted. "Do I look as if I'd make up poetry?" Bill liked to make out that he was a very tough character who despised the things of the mind. "Those are the times they spray the trees against pests."

"Well, fancy," said Charlotte. "I must say, it sounds more like poetry than pest-spraying. 'Green bud, pink bud, blossom-fall'—nice. I'm longing to see all the orchards in pink bud."

"You won't see them all in pink bud, stupid," said Bill. "Only the apples. The cherry's already out in the far orchard."

"Let's go and look at it," said Charlotte.

Midge said that she was coming too, because cherry blossom looked wonderful if you lay on the ground and looked up at it against a blue sky.

"Anything looks wonderful to you that you can look at lying down," said Charlotte.

Susan, brought up in Glasgow where the Spring, late and reluctant, had a hard job to struggle through at all, thought that lying down or sitting up, she had never in her life seen anything so beautiful as the cherry-orchards in blossom. She was content to wander through them all day long, just marvelling; or sometimes exclaiming at the beauty of an old farm-house which they would unexpectedly come upon on their wanderings, half-timbered, perhaps, settled cosily in its garden decked for Spring, beside its oasthouse of rosy brick. The only thing that she was inclined to miss about this delightful landscape was her native hills. "Honestly," she said, "it's so flat I can't believe it! I feel as if they'd dug a hole and put me in it! But I suppose you can't have everything—I mean all this and hills too. I think the scenery of Scotland is better, don't you, but I must say that Scotland doesn't have these nice wee villages——"

"We'll show you some nice villages when we're out of quarantine," promised Midge.

"And the houses. They're nearly all old and beautiful! Why doesn't Scotland have lovely old houses like these?"

"I expect the Scots were all like you, Susie," said Charlotte aggravatingly, "always rushing about interfering with their neighbours. They didn't take time to settle into this ancient peace, like the English. No sooner had they built a wee but-and-ben than some enemy clan would come rushing up and set fire to it. You lose heart after a century of two of that sort of thing and stop taking an interest in domestic architecture."

"'Interfering with my neighbours!'" Susan muttered under her breath. "As if I ever did!"

They were sitting one morning in the summer-house, enjoying the sun, sheltered from the bitter wind. Aunt Lucy had just brought out their elevenses—glasses of milk and rock-cakes—and told them to keep out of the way because Cousin Barbara was seeing that man about the orchards.

Susan bit into her second rock-cake. Cousin Barbara's rock-cakes were extra good because she put a lot of currants and orange-peel in them. Midge didn't like orange-peel and picked it all out and ranged it neatly along the edge of the plate.

"Midge, you're disgusting," said Charlotte. "Get rid of that mess at once."

"I'll eat it," said the obliging Susan. She rolled the orange-peel into a revolting little sticky ball and ate it. "What man is seeing Cousin Barbara about the orchards?" she said. She always liked to know what was going on.

"The man to buy the orchards," said Bill, who usually knew.

Susan suddenly felt sick. She put down her rock-cake and stared at Bill in horror. "Oh help, oh how awful!" she said.

Midge picked up Susan's rock-cake which was the only one left by this time and began digging the peel out of it. "Have you gone potty?" she said, but without much interest.

Susan had gone quite white. "*I* didn't know that Cousin Barbara was selling Apple-tree Farm," she wailed. "You should have told me, and I could have done something about it!"

"What *are* you raving about, Susie?" said Charlotte.

"Cousin Barbara isn't selling the *farm*, she only——" Bill began.

"But you *said* the man had come to buy the orchards," Susan interrupted.

"If you'd just let me speak," said Bill. "The man has come to buy the *apples*. Sometimes, instead of selling the apples after they're picked, fruit-growers sell the crop of whole orchards—I think they like it better——"

"Oh help, amn't I relieved!" said Susan. "I couldn't bear Cousin Barbara to sell this heavenly, heavenly place." In her relief she now had time to notice what Midge was doing. "Midge, you *cad*," she shrieked, "that's my rock-cake!"

"Well," said Midge, "you seemed to be too upset to eat it, and it was a pity to waste it."

When the wrangle over the rock-cake was settled, and Susan's mouth was, as a matter of fact, full, she said, "But there *are* no apples yet, scarcely blossom!"

"He's not buying the crop yet," said Bill, "he's only down having a look. Cousin Barbara is frightfully pleased because he's a very important buyer, only buys the best, and he has never bought from her before. His name's Pippin!"

"Oh, how sweet!" said Midge.

But Susan was anxious again. "Well, I wish I'd known before," she said, "and we could have tidied the place up a bit—all those old apple-boxes lying around the orchards look awful."

"I expect he's seen old apple-boxes before," said Midge soothingly.

"It's very important to make a good impression," said Susan. She looked round at the peaceful garden. "We could have mown the lawn. As a matter of fact, we still could. Look at all those daisies!"

"I like daisies," said Midge. "When I have a lawn of my own I'm never going to cut the daisies."

"I believe you," said Charlotte.

"No, but couldn't we mow the lawn?" said Susan. "It wouldn't be any trouble with the motor-mower." The fact was, Susan had been itching to get her hands on the mower for some time. She just saw herself going up and down the lawns, making them smooth and velvety in even strips, one finger guiding the mower and Cousin Barbara being very pleased. "Couldn't we mow the lawn, Bill?"

The mower was very old, very noisy, very smelly and very temperamental. Bill said doubtfully, "It's not as easy as it looks. That mower's an old pig."

"Well, but Cousin Barbara allows *you* to use it," said Susan.

"Yes, but Bill is mechanically-minded," said Charlotte. "If I were you, Susie, I shouldn't touch the old pig with a barge-pole. It's practically an antique and just about ripe for a museum."

Susan said obstinately, "I've been thinking for ages that I'd like to do something to help Cousin Barbara—she has been so kind having us here."

Everybody was very much affected by this speech, but Charlotte still thought that the mower was best left alone.

"But if Bill starts it for me," said Susan, "and I just push it round, wouldn't that be all right?"

Midge opened her book. "Seems to me that you don't know when you are well off," she said. "Here we are, sitting quite peacefully, no one telling us to stop what we're doing and go and do something else, and yet you want to go and mow the lawn."

"I just want to help Cousin Barbara when she has so much to do," said Susan, "and make a good impression on Mr. Pippin if we can."

"Well," said Bill weakly, "come and see if you can work it." Perhaps he hoped that the intricate mechanism of the ancient mower would be too much for Susan to grasp. "Now look," he said, "I start it with this handle——"

"Goodness," said Susan, "like a car when the self-starter won't work."

Bill quelled her with a look, and wound the handle again: and again: and again.

"I thought you said that you started it with that handle thing?" said Susan.

"What d'you think I'm trying to do?" said Bill, red-faced.

"Sorry," said Susan. "I thought maybe you'd forgotten how to work it."

"I start it with this handle," said Bill through his teeth. He gave the handle another savage turn and the machine roared into life. It shook and throbbed as if it were alive, and desperate to be off on its business; clouds of evil-smelling smoke poured out of it; the noise was fearful. Bill was pointing to a little lever on the machine's handle; Susan knew that he was speaking because his lips were moving, but she couldn't hear one word. She grinned and shook her head and shrugged her shoulders helplessly. What with one thing and another Bill was practically black in the face by this time. He was pointing a quivering finger at the little lever and obviously yelling, but Susan still couldn't hear what he was saying. She began to giggle. Bill began to dance with impatience. Fearing for his reason, Susan pulled herself together, and solemn apart from an occasional uncontrollable snort, put her mouth right up to his ear.

She yelled with all the force of her lungs, "*I can't hear! Put the thing*—OFF!"

Just as she was saying, or rather screaming, *off*, the engine stopped. Her shout could have been heard half-way to Maidstone. Bill clapped his hand over his ear and leapt away from her. "*Susie!*" he said. "I bet you've bust my ear-drum. My ear's singing like anything!"

Susan wanted to ask him what it was singing,

but didn't think that Bill would appreciate this little joke in his present mood. "Ugh, I'm sorry, Bill," she said. "Only you'll have to tell me how to work it, and *then* start it, because when it's roaring away I can't hear you."

So Bill explained the clutch, and showed her the little lever on the handle which he called a throttle, and showed her how she would make the machine go by opening the throttle, or as Susan said, by pushing the wee thing over to the left.

"And how do I stop it?" said Susan, thinking that there was more in cutting a lawn by motor-mower than you would think—goodness, it was as bad as driving a car, worse really, because a car had a self-starter.

Bill showed her how to stop it. "Although I don't expect we'll ever get the old pig started again," he said. "I expect she thinks that's her stint over for the day."

"Ugh away," said Susan. "Go and caw the handle again. I know what to do now."

This statement proved to be slightly optimistic, but Bill wasn't to know that. Muttering, "'Caw the handle!' You and your Scottish expressions!" he wound the starting handle once more. As if she had never given anybody a moment's trouble in her existence, the old pig of a machine immediately started and stood jerking and throbbing. Looking questioningly at Bill, Susan cautiously opened the throttle a little way. Bill nodded and Susan put in the clutch and cautiously moved off. "I knew I would like it," she thought, delightedly watching the clipped grass and daisy heads dancing in the box in front of her. "I hate an ordinary lawn-mower—all that pushing—but I love this!" She guided the old pig around the lawn where the baby goslings were, along the front of the big lawn by the fir-trees, round the big rose-bed with its fringe of forget-me-nots. "Nothing to it," she called to Charlotte and Midge as she passed the summer-house, nonchalantly waving her hand. Of course Midge and Charlotte couldn't make out what she was saying on account of the old pig's noise; they exaggeratedly held their noses on account of its fumes. Susan grinned and started her second time round. Whether she somehow got above herself and became careless, or whether the old pig had had enough, would never be known—certainly Susan vowed afterwards that she didn't put a finger, not even her wee pinkie-finger, on the throttle, but whatever the reason, the old pig suddenly increased its speed.

"Close the throttle! Slow her down!" yelled Bill.

Susan could guess what he was saying; she waggled the little lever desperately. The old pig went faster. "I can't do anything," yelled Susan, "the blessed thing's stuck!"

She had to trot now to keep up with the infernal machine. Midge and Charlotte put down their books and stood up to see what was going on; Bill began to run towards Susan and her monster that had got out of hand. "Watch the goslings!" shouted Bill. "Keep away from the goslings!"

At the very same moment Susan remembered

the goslings for herself and lost her head. Nothing much could have happened if she had trotted round and round the big lawn—and the lawn would have been mown in record time. But at the thought of the goslings, reared with so much care, that she might now crush or frighten to death, she swung off into the grassy path under the pergola. At the end of this walk, with its edging of daffodils, was a rustic seat and beyond it the fruit bushes—blackcurrants and redcurrants and gooseberries. Susan who, far from guiding the old pig was now being pulled along in its wake, went charging up this grassy path, mowing as she went, the Carmichaels hot at her heels. "The seat, oh mind the seat!" yelled Bill, and plunging at the mower, tried to catch one of its handles. But somehow he got mixed up with Susan's legs and stumbled into Charlotte and Midge, who were really helpless with laughing.

Susan was hanging on to her machine like grim death; just at the seat, by a superb piece of navigation, she swung the thing to the left—and as she said afterwards, it wasn't her fault that silly old Mr. Pippin had to choose that moment to come along the path from the orchard. The machine's speed increased, and now Susan was running to keep up with it; she tripped over a bramble or something and fell flat on her face. The machine, roaring madly, careered along the path, Susan yelled, Cousin Barbara yelled, Mr. Pippin yelled—but no one seemed able to *do* anything. Mr. Pippin jumped to one side, just at the same time as Cousin Barbara had the same idea;

they crashed. The machine gave a diabolical swerve and hit Mr. Pippin square in the legs, bowled him over and then, with the firm conviction that it was really a tank, went crashing wildly into the currant bushes laying them flat right and left until it came to a stop, still roaring, against a stout gooseberry bush.

For some unaccountable reason, Mr. Pippin got it into his head that the accident to the infernal machine was all his fault. Nobody went to any lengths to disabuse him of this idea except Susan, who kept on insisting in a very dogged way that no blame attached to anyone but herself. The others murmured soothingly to him that it was quite all right, that there was no harm done to speak off, and continued to offer salves, ointments and bandages for his bruised legs. He would accept nothing except a cup of tea, and went off in his car, still apologising and telling Cousin Barbara that she should hear from him later.

"I know what that means," said Cousin Barbara pessimistically. "He'd be out of his senses if he ever put foot in this farm again. Oh, well, I expect that Griffiths, my other man, will make an offer as usual only he doesn't pay so well as Mr. Pippin——"

The old pig was rescued from the gooseberry bush, apparently none the worse, in fact if anything rather better behaved than before, not that that would be difficult. Its little jaunt seemed to have done it good, and the sum total of damage in the whole terrible affair, apart from the possible effect on Mr. Pippin, was three blackcurrant bushes and one red. The effect on Susan's nerves couldn't be calculated. She said nothing more about helping Cousin Barbara and went for a walk through the water meadows to the far woods that afternoon and was much soothed by hearing a nightingale singing in broad daylight.

CHAPTER TWO

THE GIRL WITH THE SECRET

APART FROM dish-washing and other seemingly foolproof jobs, Susan was firmly discouraged from being a help for the next day or two, and in fact she had no further opportunities for helping anyone until she and Midge were out of quarantine and Belle came back to Apple-tree Farm. Belle was Cousin Barbara's "help," but she hadn't had chicken-pox and as she had a younger brother and sister at home, Cousin Barbara had forbidden her the house until all risk of infection should be over. Belle was a dark, thin, rather sullen-looking girl of about sixteen—Charlotte's age. Susan and the Carmichaels thought her rather peculiar.

"Well, she *is*," Cousin Barbara agreed, "but I couldn't get anyone else and she works like a black and actually I think that all you people have made her shy because she isn't usually as sulky-looking as this. Not that anyone could call her a little ray of sunshine about the place, but of course I don't pay any attention to her moods. Mind you, I wouldn't be a ray of sunshine myself if I had to look after two young children and get them off to school *and* go out and do someone else's housework when I should be at school myself having fun——"

Susan thought that Cousin Barbara must have

a slightly distorted view of school if she thought it was nothing but fun, but she didn't interrupt.

"But if I try to spare her," Cousin Barbara went on, "she goes in the huff and asks if I think she can't do the work and starts cleaning flues or washing down walls until I get in a perfect fright that she'll kill herself. There's an aunt in the background somewhere, so they aren't quite alone in the world, so don't look so doleful, Susan—but I got the impression that she's in hospital or somewhere at the moment, Belle is rather vague about her, and certainly she's not at the cottage. I'm terribly sorry for Belle, but there doesn't seem to be a great deal that I can do. She's so touchy I can only just persuade her occasionally to let me give her some cake for the children's tea, and we nearly came to blows when I insisted that she must take half a dozen eggs each week for the invalid aunt. In the end I lost the argument because she makes me take a shilling off her wages for them. I've never heard of anyone so proud and independent."

The Carmichaels, especially Midge, were appalled that anyone should have to work so hard, and Cousin Barbara, who had a heart as soft as butter, sighed and agreed and said that sometimes she felt that she couldn't bear to have her working there any more, but that in her queer way Belle seemed to like it at Apple-tree Farm, and that if she didn't employ her somebody else would probably take advantage of her good nature and make her work even harder and pay her less—although goodness knew that she didn't pay her as much as she would like to, only as much as she could afford.

Susan immediately decided that there was a Mystery about Belle, that she had a secret, and she told Charlotte and Midge as much when next they were on their own.

Charlotte said impatiently, "Oh, for goodness' sake, Susie——!"

"Why should there be a mystery about her?" said Midge, humouring her. "Although I must say that anyone working away like that and not going wrong in the mind must be a bit of a mystery."

"I'm sure it would astonish you to learn, Midge," said Charlotte, "that some people don't mind work. In fact they like it."

"Glory," said Midge.

"Well of course there's a mystery about her," Susan went on doggedly, ignoring the other two. "For one thing," she said, "I'm sure that her name's not Belle."

"Why shouldn't it be Belle?" said Midge. "Short for Isabel."

"Well," said Susan, "I called her Belle the other day when she was washing-up and I was drying. I spoke to her three times before she answered."

"She didn't hear you," said Midge.

"She didn't understand your Scottish accent," said Charlotte.

"Ugh away, you cheeky thing," said Susan, speaking in a very exaggerated Glasgow drawl, "it wouldny be easy tae pit much accent intae the wor-r-rd 'Belle.' And besides," she went on in her more normal voice, "she must have heard me because I was standing two inches away from her left ear. Besides, when she *did* eventually realise that I was speaking to her she jumped about two feet in the air and blushed madly!"

"But everybody else gets an answer when they call her Belle," said Charlotte.

"I know that," said Susan. "Because she's usually on her guard. But I happened to catch her off her guard. Besides, she doesn't look like a ' Belle.'"

"What does a ' Belle ' look like?" said Charlotte.

"Do people always look like their names?" Midge inquired idly.

"Ugh, yes," said Susan confidently. "You look exactly like a midge."

"And what d'you imagine a midge looks like?" said Charlotte. "I never got intimate enough with one to see. I was always too busy trying to slap the nasty things to death."

"Ugh, you know," said Susan, "skinny little things with big eyes. At least, I don't suppose they really look like that, but that's what I think they look like. And that's what Midge looks like."

"And Charlotte?" said Midge. "D'you think she *looks* like a Charlotte?"

"Well, of course she does," said Susan, who was sturdy and dark and rosy-cheeked and who admired Charlotte's looks enormously. "Tall and fair and sort of cool——"

"Cool!" cackled Midge. "That's a good description of perhaps the worst-tempered member of the family!"

"She may not act cool," said Susan, feeling slightly goaded by this time, "but she looks cool."

Charlotte, who was rather liking the idea of herself as tall and fair and cool, said, "Of course she's right about names suiting people. She suits Susan."

"Yes," agreed Midge, "I always see a Susan as a sort of person bumbling along, like a bluebottle against a window—a lot of noise and not getting anywhere in particular——"

At this description of herself Susan felt she could do no less than push Midge into the ditch —they were walking along the lane which ran down one side of the apple-orchards—and as the ditch happened to be full of water this created quite a diversion. Midge pulled Susan in after her and they splashed about wildly for a little until Charlotte told them peremptorily to get out and stop fooling about. Midge and Susan sat on the bank and took off their Wellington boots and emptied the water out of them. They were very uncomfortable to put on again, but Charlotte said that it served them right and the boots would take ages to dry.

"No, but honestly, Susie," Charlotte went back to the attack when they were all proceeding in an orderly manner along the road again and Wendy had been persuaded that there really was nothing of interest in the ditch, "you do think up the dottiest ideas. I expect you've still got a fever after your chicken-pox. Or a Spring fever."

"Yes, Susie, my pet," said Midge, "*do* leave poor

Belle in peace. I know that you're itching to help her——"

"Me help her!" squeaked Susan. "I wouldn't help her or interfere with her—or anyone—if it was the last thing I did. You know quite well that I've had enough of that sort of thing. I'm never going to be even *interested* in anyone for the rest of my life——"

Which made it all the more astonishing that she continued to hang round Belle when she had nothing else to do, trying, as unobtrusively as possible, to extract her life history from her. But she got absolutely no change out of Belle, who quite skilfully and politely evaded all her hints and told her exactly nothing. Susan tried to make out that this alone was a suspicious circumstance, but Midge said nonsense, lots of people didn't like other people quizzing them, and Susan said no more.

"Now that you little dears are out of quarantine," Cousin Barbara said after lunch that day when they were all in the drawing-room, "I'm going to take you visiting. Lucy, d'you remember Evelyn Gardiner at school——"

She was interrupted by a tremendous crash from the fireplace where Belle, having staggered in bearing an enormous basket of logs, had just dropped the lot.

"Belle, you are naughty!" said Cousin Barbara.

"I'm terribly sorry, Mrs. Trent," said Belle, embarrassed and blushing, "they slipped."

"Oh, I don't mean for dropping them," said Cousin Barbara, on her knees by the fire helping

Belle to stack the logs up, "but I've told you a hundred times not to carry so many at once."

"I wish you'd let me help you, Belle," grumbled Bill, "I love bringing in logs and I always do it at home."

"Good idea," said Cousin Barbara. "You can be the log boy, Bill."

Belle went out, and Cousin Barbara picked up her knitting. "What was I talking about?" she said.

"About going visiting," said Susan, who dearly loved going about and seeing into other people's houses.

"Oh yes," said Cousin Barbara. "Lucy, d'you remember Evelyn Gardiner at school?"

"Good gracious, yes," said Aunt Lucy. "I haven't heard of her for *years*!"

"She has been abroad," said Cousin Barbara. "She went to America when she left school—her mother was American, you know—and she has been there ever since, but she and I always wrote to each other. She got married out there about five years ago and quite recently her husband was transferred to London and of course she got in touch with me and I was able to tell her about an awfully nice house for sale at Farthing Green. She's done it up and simply beautifully—they're rolling in money."

"The Gardiners always were," said Aunt Lucy. "What happened to the elder sister? What was her name—Anne, or Anna or something?"

"Oh, my dear," said Cousin Barbara, "she died! Or was killed, rather. She married a farmer I think in Africa, and they were both shot by terrorists! It was dreadful!"

Susan nearly fell off her chair. "Shot! Africa!" she cried. "But Mummy and Daddy are in Africa!"

"I don't think you need worry, Susan," said Cousin Barbara. "Africa is a big place, and this happened miles from where your mummy and daddy are."

"It's a very sad story," said Aunt Lucy.

"'Mm," said Cousin Barbara. "There were three children too, who had been sent away for safety, and Evelyn's rather put out because she has lost track of them."

"Lost track of the children!" Aunt Lucy interrupted in amazement. "How could an aunt lose track of the children?"

"Well, apparently she and Anna had quarrelled —or rather she and Anna's husband had quarrelled Seemingly he was a queer, proud hard man——"

"Why on earth did she marry him?" Aunt Lucy interrupted again.

"Well, look, Lucy," said Cousin Barbara patiently, "I'm only telling you what Evelyn told me!"

"Sorry, sorry!" Aunt Lucy said, grinning.

"Anyway, she did marry him. He was a queer fish, Evelyn says, she couldn't stand him. He had married a girl with money, but he was determined no one would be able to cast it up at him and he wouldn't let her spend a penny of her money even if they were starving. They didn't actually starve, but it was touch and go."

"What a silly way to behave!" said Susan, who had been listening agog to this interesting story. "The money should have belonged to both of them after they were married."

"I'd like to see any husband telling *me* what to do with my money," said Charlotte fiercely.

Cousin Barbara laughed. "Oh, but poor Anna Gardiner wasn't militant like you, Charlotte," she said. "She was always a sweet docile little thing. However, she did apparently stick out about the children's education and did insist that they went to decent schools——"

"But Cousin Barbara," said Susan, her dark eye sparkling, "are these children really *lost*? Wouldn't it be *great* to find them!"

"I don't suppose they really are," said Cousin Barbara. "Three children must be rather difficult to lose. But it is true that Evelyn Gardiner wasn't told about her sister's death—she heard about it in a roundabout way quite by chance after she came to England, and when she wrote to Africa to find out about the children she was told that they had gone to England to stay with relations. Well, *she* thought that she was the only relation that they had, but she supposes they're with some connections of their father's and she so far hasn't been able to trace them. Her lawyers in London are doing their best, because she wants the children as she hasn't any of her own——"

"And she'd adopt them, and they'd live happily ever after!" breathed the romantic Susan.

"Oh, I don't know," said Midge, grinning, "aunts aren't all they're cracked up to be——"

"Get along with you, you cheeky monkey," said Aunt Lucy.

"So I thought I'd ring up and suggest going over to see Evelyn this afternoon if you'd like to," went on Cousin Barbara. "Farthing Green isn't far—about seven miles away—I'll take you in the old boneshaker. Its days are numbered, I fear, but it'll just about hold together for a bit. I think I must see if I can hire bicycles for you youngsters by the way; it would be nice for you to see something of the country round about now that you're free from infection. But we'll take the car this afternoon."

"Cousin Barbara," said Bill, "*must* I go out to tea? I was going to watch the men spraying this afternoon."

"No, you needn't, Bill," said Cousin Barbara, "but Mrs. Forester's house is an old mill-house and the stream still goes underneath the mill!"

"Oh, does it?" said Bill, thinking that that was different. "How grand to live on top of a stream!"

The girls went to get ready. "D'you know what I think? Something ought to be done about finding those children," Susan said, opening the door. "Wouldn't it be—oh, *sorry*, Belle, I didn't see you——"

"And I suppose you think you're just the person to do it?" said Midge as they went upstairs. "Well, I don't quite see where you come in on this, Susie my pet. Nor what you can do that the lawyers in London can't do."

"Oh, lawyers! Pooh!" said Susan, but she spoke in an abstracted sort of way. When they had climbed their own steep little secret stairs and Midge and she were in their room, she shut the door with great care. "Midge!" she whispered. "I think that Belle was listening at the door!"

"Oh *nonsense*, Susie," said Midge, leaning her arms on the window sill as usual and gazing out. "People don't, you know."

"Well, but you saw how I nearly knocked her down!" said Susan.

"You were going out, and she was coming in, and you met," said Midge. "What a suspicious mind you've got!"

"Ugh well, I think it was jolly queer," said Susan, changing her shoes. "Midge, get *on*, you owl, or you'll never be ready——"

CHAPTER THREE

ROBBERY AT FOLDING MANOR

THEIR WAY that afternoon led through orchards, bright with pear and cherry and plum blossom, and through hop-fields where the hops behind tall hedges were beginning to creep up the long strings prepared for them by the stilt-men. Farthing Green, when they came to it, left Susan almost— *almost*—speechless with delight. "But, but, but," she stammered, "it's got everything!"

Cousin Barbara very obligingly drove at a snail's pace through the charming village, past the old cottages, half-timbered or of rosy brick past the pretty gardens by the stream, past the green with the old church and prim Georgian houses round it and a little pond, daffodil-fringed, in the middle. A little farther on, a bigger, swifter stream flowed under the village street; a little rough road turned off by the stream and old twisted cottages crowded along it, their gardens, full of violets and primroses and daffodils, running over the river's bank. Cousin Barbara stopped the car. "There's the Mill-House," she said, pointing to a dignified grey Georgian house which looked down the rough road. Beside it stood the old mill, of white-painted weatherboard and sure enough, underneath it ran the mill stream.

Bill was delighted. "I'll bet you could swim right underneath," he said, jigging up and down in the car, "or go underneath it in a boat although I bet the current would be pretty fierce, I'll bet you could. D'you think Mrs. Forester will let me try, Cousin Barbara?"

"Not in this cold weather, I shouldn't think," said Cousin Barbara. "Look, Lucy, I thought we'd go and have a peep at the little antique shop first that I was telling you about, where I got the old maps——"

"Oh *yes*!" cried Aunt Lucy with enthusiasm. "I do want to see those maps, I love them."

Bill sighed. "Antiques!" he snorted. "When there's a *river* going under a *house*!"

Charlotte and Midge sighed a little too. They feared that one of Aunt Lucy's periodic crazes was about to be born. "I suppose we get all the pictures ripped off our walls *again*," Charlotte murmured to Midge and Bill, "and have maps put up instead."

"I shouldn't mind real maps," said Bill, "real maps are very interesting. But not those potty things that Cousin Barbara has with dolphins sporting about. And the spelling! Potty."

"I didn't think you would recognise anything queer about the spelling, young Bill," said Midge. "I think the maps are nice. 'Specially the strange and fanciful fish."

Cousin Barbara was talking to Aunt Lucy. "It's not so much antiques as old china that Miss Frame has in her shop," she said.

Charlotte pricked up her ears. Midge and Susan

looked at each other expressively. Midge said that Charlotte needn't talk, she was just as bad as Aunt Lucy; but as Susan, who loved shops, said, an old china shop was better than no shop at all, and she rather wanted to see the sort of thing that Charlotte liked, and the prices, so that she could begin to help her to buy some.

Cousin Barbara parked the car, and they walked along the village street for a little way. The Red Lion stood solidly on one side, overlooking the river. On the other side was a cottage of white weather-boarding, built so near the pavement that you could look right into the little low windows.

"Ugh, did you ever see anything so sweet!" cried Susan, peering in through the windows.

"That's Miss Frame's cottage," said Cousin Barbara. "Perhaps she'll let you see inside, Susan, if she takes a fancy to you——"

"And then you won't need to break your neck trying to peer in," said Midge.

"The shop is just here," said Cousin Barbara, pointing to another little building of weather-boarding with a nice old wrought-iron lamp hanging over the low doorway. "I don't think that there will be room inside for all this crowd."

"Oh, but look!" cried Charlotte. "The windows are full of old china! *I* must go in!"

Bill was the only one who didn't seem determined to get inside, so the others crowded in, with Aunt Lucy fussing a little and begging them to be careful and not to go knocking anything over by mistake, because *she* couldn't afford to pay for breakages in valuable old china.

A little woman came running over from the cottage. She was very tiny, to match her shop, and to match her shop also she looked like a Dresden shepherdess, with a pink and white complexion and silver hair. In her little quick and bird-like way she greeted Cousin Barbara and Aunt Lucy enthusiastically, and then she apologetically moved Susan off the mat on which she was standing just inside the door, too nervous to move on account of all that precious china. "*If* you don't mind, my dear, *over* this way a little, that's right," she twittered. "You see, when you stand on that mat it rings a bell over in the cottage and my partner's over there doing the books and he'll think it's customers——"

Susan leapt off the mat in confusion. "Ugh, I'm sorry!" she cried. "But what a *great* idea! I must tell Bill. Bill!" she called. "Bill! Come and look at this!"

Bill, who had an affection for gadgets of all kinds and liked rigging them up at home, was pleased to hear about the bell and went over to the cottage and stood listening at the door while Susan stood on the mat, until Madge, remembering Miss Frame's partner doing the books, made them stop.

Charlotte was having the time of her life looking at the old china and coveting a china poodle which she said was Rockingham and which cost five guineas. Aunt Lucy and Cousin Barbara and Miss Frame were turning over old maps, Aunt Lucy becoming more and more enthusiastic.

"*I* didn't know you had a partner, Miss Frame," said Cousin Barbara idly.

"Oh yes, Mrs. Trent," said Miss Frame, "for about a year now. He's my nephew and really more my assistant than my partner but I call him that to encourage him. The maps and those little Victorian water-colours and the flower prints were his idea. He frames them himself and they've been a very good line, I must say, a very good line. The *only* good line really," she sighed, "because no one seems to have money for old china these days. They have money for that hideous mass-produced stuff you can buy at the stores, but not for the beautiful old china when every piece was a work of art, and if things don't pick up soon, I may have to close down——" and her little pink and white face puckered up and looked like a crumpled rose-leaf.

"Oh, don't say that!" said Cousin Barbara. "I shouldn't like to think of Farthing Green without its little china shop."

"Oh, it would be a *shame* to give up this darling little shop," murmured Susan, "we must do something about that! I wish I could buy something. I love that flowery jug——"

"Which jug?" said Charlotte.

"That one," pointed Susan, "the Coalport one."

Midge and Charlotte looked at each other, and when Miss Frame had a moment to spare from the two map-enthusiasts, Charlotte said, "How much is that jug, please, Miss Frame?"

"Oh, I'm afraid it's nine guineas," said Miss Frame in distress.

"Oh!" said Charlotte, damped. "It's beautiful. Is it Coalport?"

"Yes, Coalport," said Miss Frame, and turned up the jug to show Charlotte the mark.

Charlotte and Midge were dumbfounded at Susan's knowledge, but Susan laughed and said, "Ugh, I know Coalport, it's the only one I do know because Mummy has a Coalport tea-set that belonged to her great-grandmother—our great-great-grandmother. I can remember her showing me the little flowers in the bottom of the cups as long as I can remember anything."

Nevertheless, Charlotte, who had been setting herself up as the authority on china, was still impressed.

Cousin Barbara and Aunt Lucy eventually tore themselves away from the maps, and the whole party went up the lane to the Mill-House.

"Cousin Barbara," said Susan, "surely Miss Frame won't have to give up that sweet wee shop?"

"Well, I think she's finding that times are pretty hard," said Cousin Barbara. "Of course, she's a poor shopkeeper really, much too tender-hearted and impractical. She'll knock pounds off for someone whom she thinks is a deserving customer, and if she doesn't like the look of a would-be customer she has been known to refuse to sell a favourite piece of china even if offered three times its value. There's one story that she hid a little Chelsea scent-bottle from a tactless American, but when he broke down and cried at not getting it.

she decided that he was deserving after all and let him have it and knocked two pounds off the price."

"She sounds daft," said Susan.

"No, she's not daft," Cousin Barbara said, "but it's no way to do business."

Susan privately thought that Cousin Barbara was a fine one to talk, for her own reputation for softheartedness was pretty considerable. Susan also thought that something would have to be done about Miss Frame—she would mention it to Midge later. Not, of course, that *she* had any intention of helping her.

And now they were at the Mill-House, which delightfully came up to expectations. Mrs. Forester, who was very nice and very pretty and had a slight American accent, sent them into the mill to amuse themselves, and told them not to climb on to the old mill-wheel which was absolutely rotten with age and liable to collapse at any moment, but otherwise laid no restrictions on them; and they explored all over the mill which was big and shadowy, with bits of derelict machinery left in it, and on the ' ground ' floor they could peer through the floorboards and watch the stream rushing underneath, and they could hardly hear themselves speak for the noise of it. Then they went outside and followed the stream through the garden until it rushed right under the mill, and Bill of course fell in, but only up to his knees, and Mrs. Forester gave him a pair of Mr. Forester's socks which had shrunk to put on, but she hadn't any shoes which had shrunk,

so he had to go about in his stocking-feet which
was a great treat for him.

There was a touching reunion between Aunt
Lucy and Mrs. Forester, who had last seen each
other as long-legged schoolgirls nearly twenty
years before. Susan would have liked to tackle
Mrs. Forester on the subject of her lost relations
right away, but unfortunately didn't have an
opportunity; she had to content herself with the
excitements of the mill-stream and the delights
of the lavish tea which Mrs. Forester had thought-
fully provided.

"To-morrow," thought Susan, "I will really get
to work on this mystery and start to clear it up."

But the next day brought forth another mystery
which quite diverted the interest of Susan and the
Carmichaels from long-lost nieces—not that the
Carmichaels' interest needed much diverting;
they were altogether too lukewarm, Susan considered, on the subject of long-lost nieces. "Don't
you want to find them?" she asked Midge.

"Well, it would be *nice*," Midge admitted, "but
don't you think it's a little unlikely? You know,
Susie, considering you're a Scot, who are generally
considered to be very sensible people, I sometimes
think you're definitely lacking in commonsense."

"Well," said Susan, "you're definitely lacking in
imagination and that's worse——"

"Scots wha hae!" Bill interrupted. "Look at
this piece in the *Kent Messenger*!"

THE MAD COLLECTOR STRIKES AGAIN

the headline said dramatically, and then went on:

A daring robbery took place at Folding Manor, Folding, near Maidstone, last night, when the unique Folding Letter was stolen.

The Folding Letter is, of course, the letter written to a Master Henry Folding by Shakespeare, and signed by him.

Its discovery by Miss Folding some years ago among old family papers which were thought to be of no value, was one of the literary finds of our time. Hitherto, only seven of the reputed signatures of Shakespeare had been accepted as genuine. Three of these are on legal documents, now in the Public Record Office, the Guildhall Library and the British Museum. The other three are on the sheets of Shakespeare's will in Somerset House; and the seventh was discovered in 1943 on the title-page of a book in the Folger Library in Washington. No other document in Shakespeare's own hand is known to exist.

As it would be impossible to dispose of such a priceless relic in the open market, it is believed that the robbery must be the work of the Mad Collector, as he has come to be called, who in the last year has been thought responsible for a series of thefts of Elizabethan manuscripts in country houses in Kent, among which were the robberies at Pens Place in February, and Cleve Castle last month.

None of the lost manuscripts have been recovered or heard of again, and it is believed that they have been stolen for the secret gratification of some private collector, or smuggled abroad and sold to some unscrupulous collector there.

Bill always took a great interest in robberies and such things because one of his greatest friends at home was a young policemen called Joe. The Mad Collector filled him with excitement; indeed everybody was excited—why, Folding Manor was only a mile away—they passed it every time that they went to Folding village to buy sweets or to Farthing Green!

Susan's eyes sparkled. "Now that would be something," she said, "to catch the Mad Collector!"

"You're right," said Midge sardonically. "Something like a miracle."

"Well worth your while too, Susie," said Charlotte. "The robbery's in the London papers too, and there's a piece about a reward for the recovery of the Folding Letter. Listen: FIVE THOUSAND POUNDS REWARD. Messrs. Burnett and Brown of 15 Bedford Row, offer the above reward for any information leading to the recovery of the sixteenth century letter known as the Folding Letter, stolen from Folding Manor, Folding, Kent, on April 9th; and of other manuscripts stolen from Cleve Castle, Marden, Kent, on March 6th——"

"Five thousand pounds!" cried Susan. "Wouldn't that be great! I always thought it was a nice easy way to make money, to win one of those rewards offered for lost property!"

"Sure," said Midge. "Easy. All you have to do is find the lost property. Nothing to it."

Cousin Barbara had seized the paper from Bill and was avidly scanning the account. "I remember when the letter was discovered," she murmured, "there was a tremendous to-do—the experts all got very excited and made microscopic tests and chemical tests and photographic tests and goodness knows what other tests. They looked at it under ultra-violet light and infra-red light and compared it with the known signatures, and in the end they decided it was Shakespeare's writing—the paper was right and the ink was right."

"But it *couldn't* be, could it?" said Aunt Lucy. "Only seven genuine signatures and then a whole letter to turn up!"

"Well," said Cousin Barbara, "the scholars and the palaeographers or whatever you call them—you know, the people who study old writings and inscriptions—decided it *was*. Apart from anything else, the Folding ancestor to whom the letter was written and among whose papers it was found, had been apparently stage-struck and had gone to London to try to be an actor, and it was a family tradition that he had acted at the Globe Theatre——"

"And Shakespeare was at the Globe before it was burnt down!" said Charlotte.

"Ugh, I'm sure the letter was from Shakespeare!" said Susan, adding her voice to that of the experts. "What an exciting discovery! Oh, we *must* find it!"

"Oughtn't it to have been in a museum or some place like that?" said Charlotte.

"Well, I suppose it ought, as it turns out," said Cousin Barbara, "but it was reckoned to be safe enough at Folding Manor because no one could ever sell such a thing even if they did steal it."

"D'you know, Miss Folding, Cousin Barbara?" said Susan, hoping to get in on this thrilling event on the ground floor.

"Well, hardly at all," Cousin Barbara admitted. "I've met her at the Rural Institute meetings and she usually opens the local fêtes and flower-shows."

Susan and Bill didn't consider this quite good enough for getting inside information about the robbery, so they wrote Cousin Barbara off as a dead loss, and began making plans for proceeding at once to the scene of the crime. Midge and Charlotte thought that this was a pretty boring way to spend a morning, but as it was a dull and cloudy morning anyway, and as Folding Manor was on the way to Folding where they hoped to hire some bicycles, they agreed to go, hoping that neither Susan nor Bill would make idiots of themselves.

Their way led along a quiet country road, first between orchards in pink bud, then by a slow-moving stream where, on a little wooded island, a swan was sitting on what looked like an untidy bundle of sticks but which was presumably a nest. Bill would have lingered to watch developments, but nobody seemed to think that this was a good idea so they walked on, past a grove of silver birches, past a meadow with three tall trees which, Midge told Susan, were chestnut trees—the kind you ate, not the kind you played conkers with—until round the next bend they came to Folding Manor.

The house lay close to the road; it was half-timbered, many-gabled, with lattice windows, but to Susan's fury it was half-hidden behind high yew hedges of great age. Susan complained that she couldn't see a thing. Even from the gateway there was nothing to be seen but a peaceful lovely house on a peaceful spring morning.

"You wouldn't think there had been a daring robbery *there* last night," said Susan.

"There isn't even a policeman," said Bill, disgusted.

They couldn't hang about the gate for ever—Charlotte wouldn't let them for one thing. They walked round the high hedge to the back entrance, where everything was, if anything, more peaceful than at the front. Then they walked back again. Charlotte began to show signs of boredom and became more interested in a rather ugly big house on the other side of the road which had, surprisingly enough, a moat round it on which a swan was idly swimming.

"I expect this is the father swan gadding about," said Charlotte, "while his unfortunate wife sits on the nest."

"It looked horribly uncomfortable for a nest," said Midge.

Bill said, "I wonder if he's a mute swan or a whooper—he's too far away to see his bill."

S.H.H.   C

Susan hopped up and down impatiently and said would they all stop talking about swans and get on with the detecting? How could they hope to catch the Mad Collector if they did nothing but talk about swans all the time?

"Even if we stop talking about swans," said Charlotte, "how will that help you to catch the Mad Collector?"

"Well, it won't," said Susan, "except that if we stopped talking we might *do* something——"

"Such as?" said Charlotte.

"Well——" said Susan. "Well, going up to the house, looking for clues——"

"You can count me out of *that*," said Charlotte emphatically. "And her too I should think," she added, jerking her head at Midge who having wearied of the discussion, was leaning up against a gate reading the book that she had taken out of her pocket.

"Ugh, you're a hopeless lot," said Susan. "Bill, are you coming?"

"I suppose I'd better come and look after you, Susie," said Bill, who couldn't have been kept from Folding Manor by wild horses, "we don't want you bursting in on the Squire and disgracing us."

"Me disgrace you!" said Susan.

Charlotte saw that there would be no peace until Susan and Bill had done a bit of what they were pleased to call detecting, so she sighed and said, "Hurry up then. We'll walk slowly on. Don't do anything silly."

Bill said that he knew what walking slowly on meant, and they must promise to *wait*.

"We'd better wait for the remains, I suppose," said Charlotte, and climbing on to the gate, sat there, viewing the landscape.

"Remains, what remains?" said Susan anxiously.

"Your remains," said Charlotte. "The police will kill you. Or the people in the house will see you prowling about and give you in charge. Either way we'll be disgraced and I'm mad to let you go."

Susan, looking a little alarmed, hesitated, but Bill pulled her away from Charlotte's gloomy prophecies. "How do we start?" he said. "We can't go marching up to the front door."

"Let's creep in the back," said Susan, and dropped on all fours for creeping purposes. But Bill pointed out that there didn't really seem to be any need for such dramatic measures yet, and suggested that they'd better just stroll in the back way and see what was what.

The road curved round the house at this point; the back premises were only on the other side of the hedge. Susan and Bill strolled through the gate. A drive wound round to the front of the house, through an archway of ancient yew. A tabby cat strolled across the cobbled yard to the open back door and disappeared inside. There was no other movement, no sound. "It's like a house of the dead!" whispered Susan. Suddenly there was a soft rush of wings and a ghostly shape came out of the trees and passed over their heads.

"*Bill!*" gasped Susan, clutching his arm. "*What was that?*"

"Leggo my arm, you clot," said Bill in rather a cross voice. "That jolly well hurt!"

"But *Bill!*" said Susan, still holding his arm but not quite so tightly. "It was a ghost!"

"As a matter of *fact*," said Bill, "it was a white owl."

Susan laughed shakily, disbelievingly. "Ugh, Bill, it was not!" she said. "Owls don't fly about at ten o'clock in the morning."

"Neither do ghosts, for that matter," said Bill. "Owls do it oftener than ghosts."

"Well," said Susan, rather put out, because she had had a fright, "the whole thing is, the place is too quiet! They should all be rushing about looking for clues after a burglary!"

"I expect they've all gone back to bed to recover," said Bill. "After all, Sir Hubert's frightfully old. About sixty, Cousin Barbara said."

"Goodness!" said Susan. "Older than Aunt Lucy! She'll be thirty-nine on her birthday."

"Let's creep round to the front," said Bill.

They advanced cautiously towards the arch of yew. "Really," said Susan, "I'm not surprised that they've had a burglary. We could burgle the place ourselves——" Suddenly she made a clutch at Bill's arm again. This time he was too quick for her and she only grasped a handful of jersey. "Look at that!" she said, pointing dramatically.

"Look at what?" said Bill. "That patch of mud?"

"There, in the middle of the patch!" said Susan. "That's a clue!"

"Nonsense," said Bill. "That's the mark of a bicycle tyre."

Close under the yew hedge was a patch of wet mud, and across the middle of it was a clear and beautiful print of a bicycle tyre, and a new tyre at that. Susan and Bill bent over to examine it.

"That's certainly a clue," said Susan. "The Mad Collector came on a bicycle!"

"Really, Susan," said Bill, disgusted by such detection. "How can you possibly tell? It might be the postman's bicycle or the paper-boy's."

"No," said Susan positively. "The postman and the paper-boy would go to the back door."

"Oh," said Bill. "Well—perhaps they would. But it might be Sir Hubert's bicycle."

"Ugh away," said Susan. "The Squire would be riding a Rolls-Royce, not a bicycle."

"Not if he's a poor squire," said Bill. "Or it might be that one of the servants has a bicycle."

"The servants wouldn't ride it round to the front either," said Susan. "No, it's a clue, definitely. Could you draw the marks on a piece of paper so that we'd know them if we saw them again?"

"I could if I had a piece of paper," said Bill.

Much delving in pockets produced a very small stump of pencil but no paper. Susan fished out a toffee paper, rolled into a tight little ball from the corner of her blazer pocket. It wasn't easy drawing a sketch of the tyre-marks with such inadequate implements. Bill smoothed out the toffee paper as best he could on his knee, and drew —watched intently by Susan.

It was the sound of heavy breathing which made them look up eventually. There, right beside them, watching their efforts with deep interest, stood a fat policeman.

Susan gave a great jump of terror and yelped. Bill also jumped. The fat policeman bent over and stared at the ground. "Got anything good there?" he said eagerly.

"Yes!" said Susan.

"No!" said Bill, both together.

"It's a clue!" said Susan.

"'Tisn't!" said Bill. "It's only the mark of a bicycle tyre. One of the servant's bicycles. Or an errand-boy."

The fat policeman put his hands on his knees and breathed more heavily than ever as he bent over and gazed at the mark of the tyre. "Mr. Benson's the butler," he said, "and he's over seventy and hasn't ridden a bicycle since the penny-farthing days. His wife's the housekeeper and she has never ridden a bicycle in her whole life as far as I know. And I ought to know because she's my auntie. So I don't think as she's likely to start now. And the only other servant is old Polly Downs from Folding who comes in to oblige every morning and couldn't ride a bicycle because of her rheumatics, like. Me own bicycle's at the back door where it should be. No, reckon you've got a clue there all right, all right!"

Susan beamed delightedly at him. This was the nicest policeman that she'd ever met, not always trying to put a damper on the efforts of the gifted amateur. "Are you in charge of the case, inspector?" she said.

The fat policeman's open face clouded over. "Well," he said reluctantly, "in a manner of speaking, not exactly. That nosey-parker inspector from Maidstone came over first thing, and young Sergeant Botting from Folding managed to push himself forward as usual. As if he'd ever do any good—all la-di-da and rushing about on a motor-bike."

"Of course not!" Susan agreed enthusiastically. "Oh, we'll help you Mr.—er—er——"

"Bristow, miss, Constable Bristow."

"Why, you're the Paddocks constable!" said Bill.

"That's right! The constabulary is right there in that row of cottages beyond Mrs. Trent's big orchard. Gets me milk regular from Mrs. Trent. Seen you about a dozen times in the last week or two! Chicken-pox, wasn't it?"

Bill had previously listened with horror to Susan giving away all their clues to the first stray policeman that came along. Now that Mr. Bristow had established himself as Paddocks' very own policeman, Bill was more than willing to co-operate with him. Mr. Bristow was sadly telling Susan that now they were talking of calling in Scotland Yard, and confessing that so far there hadn't been the sight or smell of a clue except that the robbery was the work of the Mad Collector all right, all right—nothing but the Folding Letter taken, although why anyone should go for to steal a little old dirty bit of paper was more than he could understand. He'd seen it in its glass case often when he was calling on the Squire about them there poachers that had been around, gipsies, he reckoned and he'd told the Squire so, but that Sergeant Botting he thought different of course, and he hadn't thought it worth a row of beans, although he dared say the Squire set more store by it, it being what you might call an heirloom like and Miss Folding finding it and all.

When Bill could get a word in edgeways, he asked when the robbery had actually taken place, and Mr. Bristow told him at eight o'clock the previous evening when the family were at dinner —the Mad Collector just walked in and helped himself like.

"What cheek!" said Bill. "Please, Mr. Bristow, may I come over and see you to-morrow and find out if there's any news? And perhaps you could tell us a bit more about the Folding Letter—what it looks like and so on."

"Come and welcome, Master Bill, and it looks like any dirty old piece of paper and the writing that queer—but I've got the size of it written down somewhere. It would be a fine thing if we could find it between us!" said Constable Bristow, his honest face gleaming.

Susan protested that any help *she* could give would be given. Bill didn't know whether to warn Mr. Bristow about Susan's help but on the whole thought that Mr. Bristow was old enough to look after himself. But what they must do now was get back to the others or Charlotte would be in a panic. Susan, who had been planning that Mr. Bristow should lead her to Sir Hubert there and then in order that she might get more information from him, reluctantly allowed herself to be dragged away, but assuring Constable Bristow that he need have no fear, they would certainly help him to find the Mad Collector—if for no other reason than to spite the la-di-da sergeant from Folding.

Charlotte's surprise was extreme when Susan and Bill reappeared with a stout policeman with whom they were obviously on the best of terms. Susan and Bill, looking smug, said good-bye affectionately to the stout policeman and walked over to Charlotte who was still sitting on the gate.

"Did you see that policeman?" said Bill. "Well, he's the Paddocks policeman. He knows Cousin Barbara quite well, in fact he gets his milk from her. _They_ haven't found a single clue. The Mad Collector walked in and helped himself to the Folding Letter out of its glass case when they were all at dinner, and walked out again. The only thing is, we have discovered that he came on a bicycle."

"On a bicycle!" Charlotte exclaimed in disgust.

"Mr. Bristow thinks so too," said Susan quickly, anxious to show that they had some solid support for their theory. "That was Mr. Bristow you saw us talking to."

"Well but really, a bicycle!" said Charlotte. "Is that likely?"

"Well," said Bill, "we found a tyre mark in a patch of mud, and as nobody at Folding Manor has a bicycle and most of them can't even ride a bicycle because they're so old, we think it's a clue. But we're not going to say a word about it."

"I should think not," said Charlotte. "Who ever heard of a burglar using a bicycle?"

"I don't see why the Mad Collector shouldn't use a bicycle," said Susan. "He's not an ordinary burglar. He might be an eccentric professor or anything, and professors quite often ride bicycles. A bicycle would make a lot less noise than a car stopping and starting."

"Yes, I suppose so," Charlotte said doubtfully. "But if he were disturbed at his burgling he could never hope to get away on a bicycle."

"He could pretend to be an innocent passer-by and help in the chase," said Susan. "No one would *expect* a man on a bicycle to be the Mad Collector."

"I think you've got a point there," said Bill.

"But here's another thing," said Charlotte. "If the Mad Collector does his burgling by bicycle, that must mean that he lives somewhere near. I can't see even an eccentric professor cycling down from London every time he wanted to do a little burgling!"

Susan looked alarmed and glanced over her shoulder as if the Mad Collector might be behind the hedge. Then she laughed a little and blushed, hoping nobody had noticed.

"All the robberies being in Kent, and this part of Kent, bears that out," said Bill. "I really do think we're on the right lines——"

"On the right lines!" said Charlotte scornfully. "All you have to do is find the right bicycle out of the thousands of bicycles in Kent! Anyway, let's get on now, for goodness' sake or it'll be to-morrow morning before we get *our* bicycles."

So they prodded Midge into activity—she had been lying on the grass by the side of the road, reading, throughout the discussion—and they went on to Folding, which was about half a mile farther on.

Folding was another delightful village, in a different style from Farthing Green. A wide village street led down the hill from the Walnut Tree, with thatched cottages of brick and bright-painted weather-boarding placed higgledy-piggledy along it, varied by a gracious eighteenth century house, and leading past the church built on a little rise to an ancient narrow bridge, which spanned flat meadows and the slow-moving river. Susan was pleased to discover a butcher's shop built actually on the bridge, and in the church-yard a great magnolia tree in bloom, which filled her with wonder, as she had never come across such marvels in her bleak northern home.

Half-way down the street they found the man who hired out bicycles and who turned out to be the smith, and got themselves suited and were able to watch a horse being shod at the same time. Susan shook the others a little by suddenly asking the smith if he sold bicycle tyres?

"Yes, I do, now and then," said the smith, "but you'll not be wanting a new tyre yet, I hope."

Susan said oh no, she wouldn't, she just wanted to look at them, and the man showed her a few hanging up in the dim recesses of the smithy.

Susan looked at each one intently to the embarrassment of the others, who eventually managed to get her away.

"What d'you think you were doing?" said Charlotte, as they thankfully mounted their new bicycles and made for Paddocks.

"I was looking at the treads," said Susan. "They were different from the Clue. I wanted to know if all bicycle treads were the same."

"Are you going to examine every bicycle tyre you see?" said Midge.

"Of course," said Susan.

"Then I don't think I'll come out with you," said Midge. "Of all the boring things. I think I'll be the kind of detective who solves the whole case without stirring from his chair."

"What do you know about it anyway," said Susan. "You were reading while we were telling Charlotte about the Clue."

"Oh, I pick things up," said Midge.

CHAPTER FOUR

INVESTIGATING BELLE

IF MIDGE picked things up, she was the only one, because Bill didn't manage to pick up anything next morning when he hurried over to the Kent Constabulary. Mrs. Bristow was delighted at having her milk delivered, but Mr. Bristow wasn't able to give Bill any more information. He read out to Bill the descriptions of the manuscripts stolen from Pens Place and Cleve Castle; Bill didn't pay much attention, but he noted down, with his horrid little stump of pencil, that the Folding Letter was six and a half inches by four.

Nobody, except Susan, seemed to be particularly interested in his detecting activities when he went back to the farm. The grown-ups were planning to go into Maidstone to do some Easter shopping, for this was Thursday and Sunday would be Easter Day. The girls were eager to go too, but Bill thought that he would stay at the farm— really, he had rather been neglecting his duties recently, and he didn't know at all how the spraying would be getting on without him.

"Aren't you coming to Maidstone to buy us a lot of lovely Easter presents?" said Midge.

"I've got your Easter presents," said Bill, looking a little self-conscious.

"Stay at home if you like, young Bill," said

Cousin Barbara. "Belle will give you some lunch. But I thought that we'd have lunch at the George and if there's anything suitable on, you children could go to the pictures and come home in the bus. *I* can't wait because I must get back to make the hot-cross buns and ice the cake."

"Oh, if you're all going to the pictures," said Bill, "that's different."

"I'll come back with you, Barbara," said Aunt Lucy. "There's always such a lot to do before a holiday."

"That will fit in very nicely," said Midge when they went to get ready, "for I don't expect that any of you remembered that it's Aunt Lucy's birthday on Wednesday, and now we'll be able to do some shopping on the quiet."

"*I* hadn't forgotten," said Susan, "only I thought it would be nice to give her one of those old maps. But they were so dear! Even those two little road maps that she liked so much were more than a pound each and I only have about ten shillings."

"Yes, I thought of the maps too," said Charlotte. "Or a bit of china."

"A bit of china!" jeered Midge. "To add to your collection, I suppose! A map is just the thing—couldn't we club together?"

"That's an idea," said Susan.

"We'll see what we have left after to-day," said Charlotte, " and get it on Saturday when we go over to spend the day with Mrs. Forester."

"That's two whole days to wait," Susan objected, "and the shop might be shut!"

"I shouldn't think it will be," said Charlotte, "these little antique shops keep open on Saturdays, and Sundays too, those are the only days they do any business. But if it's shut we can pop over on Tuesday."

"We might even go to-morrow," said Susan, "even if it is Good Friday. Only Uncle Charles will be arriving then—perhaps we'd better wait till Saturday. But if the maps are sold!"

"Stop flapping, Susie," said Midge. "The maps won't be sold. Business is bad, according to Miss Frame."

"Well, all right," said Susan; and they set off merrily for their day in Maidstone.

They enjoyed themselves very much; they did their shopping, had a very grand lunch, went to the pictures and came home on the five o'clock bus. Cousin Barbara had been busy, the cake was iced and decorated with a chocolate nest, filled with pale blue marzipan eggs, and the hot-cross buns smelt so good that she had difficulty in keeping the family from eating them immediately.

"Look here," she said at last in desperation, "I know how to get rid of you——" She hastily wrapped some buns in a clean cloth and put them in a basket. "Take these over to poor little Belle for to-morrow."

"*Another* walk!" said Midge aghast. "Just after we've walked a mile from the bus!"

"Ugh, I'd love to take them," said Susan eagerly. This was just the chance that she had been waiting for. She had been itching to get inside Belle's house and have a good look round ever since she had begun to take an interest in her, which was the moment she saw her. "We can go on our bicycles."

"Well, have tea first," said Cousin Barbara, shooing them out of the kitchen, "and maybe Midge will feel stronger by then."

"I doubt it," said Midge faintly.

However, after a quick tea, Midge did allow herself to be persuaded to go with Susan to Belle's house, which had the delightful name of Folly Cottage and was as delightful as its name, old and twisted and thatched. Behind it were apple-trees and opposite it a little wood, and farther along the lane a peaceful-looking farm formed a pleasant background with its screen of tall firs and oasthouses with their white-pointed cowls.

In the tiny garden of the cottage two children, a girl and a boy of about nine and seven, were planting seeds with deep concentration.

Midge and Susan leant over the gate. "Hallo," said Susan.

The children looked up. The boy smiled and went back to his planting; the girl, who had a wistful little face, said hallo gravely and stared at them.

"Is Belle in?" said Midge.

"Yes," said the girl, "shall I get her?"

"Ugh no, don't bother," said Susan hastily. She didn't want to be done out of her visit at this stage. "We'll just knock."

No one could have called Belle's manner welcoming. She stood at the door and glowered at them and took the basket of hot-cross buns with rather grudging thanks; and Susan would have been no nearer to seeing the inside of her house if Midge hadn't said in a faint voice, "May we come in? I'm exhausted——"

Belle hesitated and then said shortly, "Of course," and stood back.

The door led directly into a small living-room, very plainly furnished, but brightened by bowls of primroses and violets on every ledge.

"What a sweet wee room!" said Susan. "Is that a photo of your mother?" she added, indicating a small framed photograph of a sweet-faced woman, laughing and looking down at the two small children who were crawling over her knees.

"Yes," said Belle, and as if to avoid any further inquiries, she added harshly, "She's dead."

It worked all right. Susan blushed scarlet and mumbled, "Ugh, I'm *sorry*." There was an awkward little pause.

Then Midge, who had flopped into a shabby armchair, said softly, "My mother's dead too. But of course Aunt Lucy is as good as a mother, and actually I can scarcely remember my own." Belle looked slightly softened and Midge went on, "But Belle, do you live here all by yourselves, you and the two children?"

"Yes," said Belle. And then she added, " I have an aunt too, but she's—she's away at the moment."

"Glory," said Midge, admiringly. "You must have a lot to do—looking after all this and then doing Cousin Barbara's work."

"Oh, I don't mind," said Belle, and she glanced out of the window at the back where one of the apple trees was in bud. "We like it here," she said, and gave a little smile.

"Where did you live before?" Susan took advantage of the improved atmosphere to ask.

"London," said Belle. "Bloomsbury. It was horrible."

"Handy for the British Museum," said Midge vaguely.

"I say, would you like some lemonade?" Belle suddenly remembered her manners. "I made some yesterday."

So then they had quite a merry party and the children came in from their gardening and joined them. The girl, Mary, was a quiet, grave little thing, but Robert was very friendly and chattered all the time, and insisted on taking them out and showing them the bare patch of earth where he had put his seeds.

"He'll have them all dug up to-morrow to see how they're getting on," said Mary rather hopelessly, but Robert only laughed and went capering round the garden.

"Oh well, I suppose we'd better go now," said Midge.

"We'll be popping over on Easter Day," said Susan, "with—well, anyway, we'll be over to see you."

And Midge and Susan made their way homewards.

CHAPTER FIVE

HELPING MISS FRAME

THAT EVENING after supper Aunt Lucy was very indulgent and let Bill sit up a bit late with the girls. A fire of enormous logs was burning cosily in the sitting-room, and they played a card-game called Spit. This had actually nothing to do with spitting, except that, as Susan said, it made her spit with rage. It required great speed and dash and Susan was hopeless at it; she got red in the face and more and more helpless until she was eventually just waving her hands making little shrieks of disgust and watching Midge pile up the cards with quiet competence to win the game. They all got very thirsty with excitement, and eventually the children went into the kitchen to make tea for the grown-ups and cocoa for themselves.

"You know," said Susan, who had obviously been thinking of other things when she should have been thinking of Spit, "we talk about helping Miss Frame, but nobody does anything about it."

"*You're* the only one who ever talks about helping anyone," said Midge. "Pass me the tea, Susie, it's in that tin with the roses on it."

"The whole thing is," said Charlotte, a trifle smugly, "not enough people like old china."

"The whole thing *is*," said Susan, ignoring Midge, "that the shop is too much out of the way."

What Susan said was perfectly true; a narrow, unfrequented road led through Farthing Green, while a few hundred yards away a ceaseless stream of traffic roared along the main road to Folkestone and the coast.

"A good idea," Susan went on, "would be to divert some of that traffic through Farthing Green. I don't imagine that the lorries or buses would pay much attention, but some of the cars would stop at Miss Frame's dear wee shop."

"Well," said Charlotte, "why don't you dress up as a traffic cop and divert them?"

A gleam came into Susan's eye, then she said, "Ugh away, you're joking. "But," she added, the gleam re-appearing, "there are other ways of diverting traffic." As she didn't think that Charlotte would prove very sympathetic towards the scheme which had just started into her head, she said no more, but spoke to Midge and Bill later when they were going up to bed.

Bill embraced the scheme with enthusiasm. "Early to-morrow morning we must do it, to catch the Good Friday traffic—there should be lots of people on their way to the coast for the week-end," he said.

"Early?" said Midge apprehensively. "How early?"

"About six," said Bill.

"Well, that settles it," said Midge. "You can count me out."

"Ugh away, Midge," said Susan, "surely you wouldn't mind getting up early for once, to help Miss Frame?"

Midge said that she'd mind very much; but they eventually managed to persuade her, and she reluctantly allowed herself to be dragged out of bed at half-past five. How could she sleep anyway, she said, with the alarm that Susan had borrowed from Cousin Barbara shrieking in her ear?

They filled their pockets with rock-cakes from the big tin in the kitchen and with apples from the apple-house, and then they were ready to set off for Farthing Green. The village was deserted, naturally, at that time in the morning, and Susan led them to the spot where she had seen the yellow A.A. Road Diversion notices and the road-blocks like wooden triangles.

"It's rather a long way to the main road, isn't it?" said Midge. "And won't someone see us?"

Bill brought out the bundle which he had stuffed under his pullover. This proved to be the sheet off his bed. "We wrap the A.A. notice and the road-blocks in this," he said, "and no one will know what we've got."

"Ugh Bill, you're brainy," said Susan with enthusiasm, "they'll think it's a body."

"Very angular body," said Midge. "Well, come on, let's get it over."

It took them three journeys and Midge was complaining bitterly by the time they had finished; but the main road to the coast was now blocked and a real, official, yellow A.A. notice diverted the traffic through Farthing Green.

"We'll come back after breakfast and see how things are going," said Susan.

There were new-laid eggs for breakfast when the arrived back at the farm, and the hot-cross buns. Everybody had about four each, hot and dripping with butter. Even Susan was a little languid after breakfast and went out and sat on the wall in the sun by the wallflowers.

"We don't want to go back to you-know-where too soon," she said to Midge.

"I don't want to go back at all," said Midge sleepily.

But after their elevenses, which surprisingly enough they were all able to eat, Susan got restless again, and eventually she nagged Midge and Bill into returning to Farthing Green to see how their scheme was progressing.

An amazing sight met their eyes.

From one end to the other, the entire length of Farthing Green's village street was blocked with traffic. Big cars, small cars, grand cars and shabby cars were jammed in an impenetrable mass; by some incredible manœuvre, one was facing the opposite way from all the others. Susan and Midge and Bill, feeling awed, got off their bicycles and pushed them along the pavement. They certainly couldn't have pushed them along the road. As they went towards Miss Frame's the confusion, if anything, became worse—cars were mounted half on the pavement, every side turning was full of cars, the road round the green was a solid mass of cars. People were shouting, red-faced, horns were blowing, the la-di-da sergeant from Folding, looking demented, was blowing his whistle. The villagers of Farthing Green were out in a body, enjoying the spectacle.

The children lifted their bicycles over a convenient wall and edged onwards on foot. Suddenly Bill spotted Constable Bristow, calm-faced in the middle of the turmoil. They pushed their way towards him.

"Constable Bristow," yelled Bill, "what has happened?"

A great beam spread over Constable Bristow's broad face. "Didn't reckon ever to see Bank Holiday crowds like this in Farthing Green, eh?" he cried jovially. "Now madam," he said, turning to a fussed lady motorist, "it isn't a bit of good you toot-tooting away there, road's blocked, completely blocked. And I dare say you do want to get to Folkestone by lunch-time, but it won't be to-day, I reckon, not unless that there little car o' yours is a helicopter in disguise. We're clearing a way through as fast as we can, I reckon —there's Sergeant Botting down there busting his buttons trying to clear a way—yes, I agree, madam, it's downright disgraceful, that it is, but what can't be cured must be endured I says, and we'll get you to Folkestone all right, all right——"

Susan pulled his sleeve. It seemed the only way to stem Constable Bristow's eloquence. "But Constable Bristow," she said, "what *happened*?"

Constable Bristow beamed again—he hadn't enjoyed himself so much since the day Farmer Hubble's horses got into Farmer Roper's orchards and ate his prize Cox's pippins and them two at

daggers drawn for forty year as everybody knew
—Susan pulled his sleeve again. Constable
Bristow looked down at her, smiling. "Well,
some joker moved the road diversion notice from
down the bottom there and put it on the main
road and sent all the traffic through the village,"
he said. "And of course the road being up down
the bottom there and no notice to send cars round
the other way, the traffic got a bit jammed-up,
like. But it'll soon be on the move and back on
the main road again."

Susan said good-bye to Constable Bristow and
the children pushed on towards Miss Frame's shop.
"Ugh, we clean forgot that the diversion notice
was there for a purpose!" Susan said. "No wonder
that there was a wee bit of congestion!"

There was terrific activity round the Red Lion
—cars were parked along the front of it and over-
flowing into the garden—you felt that at any
moment they would overflow into the river—the
boots, the chambermaids, everybody that had two
sound legs, were rushing round serving teas and
coffees to the motorists.

"Well," said Susan, more complacently, "we've
done the Red Lion a good turn, that's one thing."

At Miss Frame's little shop the confusion was
frightful. The cars were stuck fast here nose to
tail past her shop and right up the hill towards
the main road. One thruster, not content with the
evidence of his eyes, had tried to pass the car in
front, and had only succeeded in wrecking Miss
Frame's garden gate.

"That's the way, Susie," said Midge nastily,

" help Miss Frame—knock her gate down for her. An inch farther and he'd have knocked the house down."

Susan hastily averted her eyes; but she cheered up instantly when she saw the little shop. "It's like Woolworth's!" she said delightedly. "Packed to the doors!"

Certainly there was no hope of getting inside the shop. They stood on tiptoe and jumped up and down to get a view inside, past the china and old maps in the windows. Crowds of bored motorists had invaded the shop in a body and were packed tight as sardines inside. The children caught occasional glimpses of Miss Frame and her partner, red in the face and harassed.

"There!" said Susan triumphantly. "Just as we planned!"

At that moment, the bottle-neck at the bottom of the village was cleared; the cars slowly began to move. Those stuck behind the shoppers set up a frantic hooting and Miss Frame's customers burst out of the shop like a river in spate. Susan and Midge and Bill watched them open-mouthed as they bundled into their cars and hurried on towards the coast. At the shop Miss Frame, her silver hair ruffled, sat on the step; her partner leaned up against the door, panting.

"Ugh, Miss Frame," said Susan, "what a crowd! Did you do great business?"

"Oh, good morning, children," said Miss Frame in her precise little voice. "Such a to-do! Well, no, not very good really—a nice old Derby vase, one of my better pieces, got smashed in the crush, and I'm afraid that somebody went off with a very nice Worcester plate without paying—isn't it horrid that people should be so dishonest? But we mustn't be harsh, I dare say that he just forgot and hurried off when the road became clear."

"Miss Frame, how sickening!" cried Susan. "What was he like? I'll go after him——!"

"Oh, thank you, but I'm afraid that he will have gone by now."

"Didn't you sell anything?" said Midge.

"Well, yes, I did," said Miss Frame, her pink and white face brightening, "I sold a little mug that I was never happy about. I bought it as Lowestoft but I'm sure it wasn't. Of course I told the customer so, and I let her have it very cheap, less than I paid for it, really——"

"So really," Susan said sadly, "this morning was just a dead loss?"

"Well," said Miss Frame, "it was an experience."

Susan and Midge and Bill said good-bye and crept slowly off to find their bicycles.

It took the arrival of Dr. Carmichael from London that afternoon, laden with mysterious parcels which he immediately hurried away out of sight, to cheer Midge and Bill up again, and to bring a smile to the sad face of Susan.

CHAPTER SIX

SUSAN IS INQUISITIVE

SUSAN WAS determined that, come what might, she was going to find out more about Mrs. Forester's long-lost relations when the family went over to the Mill-House to spend the day on Saturday. So after a wonderful lunch of fried chicken and lemon meringue pie with lots and *lots* of cream, when Uncle Charles and Mr. Forester, who was a big, cheery American with a twinkle in his eye, went off to play golf or something, and the Carmichaels were enjoying themselves messing about by the stream, and trying to avert Bill's falling in again, Susan hung round Mrs. Forester, asking questions. Aunt Lucy was obviously a bit fed-up with her and anxious to be rid of her, but Susan was deaf to all hints and went on hanging around.

"Mrs. Forester," she said, "no word of the nieces yet, I suppose?"

"Why no, Susan," said Mrs. Forester in her pretty voice with the slight American accent. "My lawyer is trying to get in touch with the lawyers in Africa who dealt with my sister's affairs. But you know what lawyers are and it's a slow business."

"What are their names?" said Susan. "The nieces', I mean, not the lawyers'——"

"Evelyn was the eldest, she was called after me, then Mary, and Robert."

"Susan, wouldn't you like to go out and join the others?" Aunt Lucy tried again.

"Yes, all right," Susan said reluctantly. "I just like hearing about Mrs. Forester's nieces."

"Susan is full of imagination," said Aunt Lucy rather apologetically. "I expect she has already visualised a touching reunion scene."

Susan blushed and began kicking a chair-leg with her toe, but Mrs. Forester laughed. "I'll show you some photographs of them if you like, Susan," she said. "Though I guess they're not very recent. And Barbara, I've got some that were taken that holiday you spent with us in Cornwall, do you remember? They'll make you smile—isn't it awful how ridiculous we look in old photos?"

They all crowded round the photograph albums that Mrs. Forester took out. As clues, the snaps of the children couldn't be counted as much use, as the most recent of them was six years old, but Susan did find something vaguely familiar about one of the people in the groups. She asked Mrs. Forester about her. "That's my sister, the children's mother," said Mrs. Forester.

Cousin Barbara and Aunt Lucy were shrieking over the twenty-year-old snaps. "Oh, Evelyn!" cried Cousin Barbara. "*Look* at you in this one—your hair! That was the day we went to Harlyn Bay—I've never forgotten it—it was such a wonderful day and the bay was so lovely—the rocks and the yellow sands and the blue, blue sea!

And we went on to Padstow and bought ships in bottles in that little shop, d'you remember?"

"The one I bought is over there in that corner cupboard," said Mrs. Forester.

"And who is that girl?" went on Cousin Barbara. "Isn't that the cousin or something who lived with you? What was her name?"

"Esther Groves," said Mrs. Forester, leaning over Susan and looking at the photos.

"Esther Groves, of course! What happened to her?"

"Oh, she lived with me until only about a year ago," said Mrs. Forester. "When we had grown up and were beginning to leave home a bit she lived with mother as a sort of companion, and when I got married and mother died she came to me. We had a tremendous lot of entertaining and so on to do in New York and she acted as my secretary, coped with all my mail and looked after my lists of guests—she was a boom, too— you know how untidy I am! I had a dreadful time at first after she went—couldn't find a thing! Some of the things I never did find again—for instance my birth certificate and my old passport, which was kind of awkward when I came to get another. The strange thing was, that Esther never wrote me a word, not even a postcard, after she left and went back to England."

"She was a queer girl," said Cousin Barbara. "Quite frankly I never could stand her. I always thought that sweet and gentle manner was put on. You were all very good to her."

"Oh well," said Mrs. Forester. "She was a half-cousin you know, and her parents died when she was about fifteen and left her absolutely destitute. Mother had to do something and she made her home with us after that. She *was* a bit queer, rather bitter and grudging—and she seemed to be at your *heels* all the time—she got on my nerves. I couldn't help feeling thankful when she told me that she wanted to go back to England. But I felt guilty at the same time too, because I had so much and she had so little——"

"Strange that she didn't write," said Cousin Barbara. "She probably will when she wants something."

Mrs. Forester laughed. "Oh, she wasn't as bad as that," she said. "She doesn't know that I'm in England, and of course I don't know where she is."

They went on exclaiming and laughing over the photographs, and Susan did finally have the grace to leave them to it. She wondered if Mrs. Forester would like her to find Esther Groves for her, but decided not, on the whole. She sought out her cousins and began nagging at them to go down to Miss Frame's and buy Aunt Lucy's birthday present. The Carmichaels were rather loath to leave their water pleasures, for they had found an old boat that scarcely leaked at all and were arguing over who should have first chance to go under the mill in it. However, it did seem a good opportunity to go, when Aunt Lucy was occupied within doors.

"I didn't think you'd be able to look Miss Frame in the face again," said Midge.

Susan wriggled uncomfortably. "Well, at least

we're really helping to-day," she said, "being real customers."

"How much money have we got?" said Bill, tearing himself reluctantly away from that wonderful mill-stream and wiping his hands on the seat of his trousers.

Charlotte had been appointed cashier. She took her purse out of the pocket of her skirt and counted the money. "One pound one and eleven-pence," she said.

"That means," said Midge, "that we can buy one of the old road maps that Aunt Lucy liked, and I think we should buy the one of the road from London to Hythe that shows Paddocks and Folding, because I think Aunt Lucy liked it best."

"The one that spelt Hythe, H-i-t-h," said Bill, in rather a superior voice.

Everyone agreed that the road map was the one —among the cheaper ones—that Aunt Lucy had fancied. They hurried down the little lane by the mill-stream, and round the corner to Miss Frame's shop. It was shut.

"Ugh!" cried Susan. "How sickening and maddening and disgusting and I don't like to say I told you so, but——"

"Look," said Midge mildly, "I expect that Miss Frame is over in the cottage having a cup of tea."

But although they went to the cottage and knocked and rang, and Susan obligingly went round to the front and peered in at the windows, Miss Frame didn't appear.

"We must just come back another day," said

Charlotte. "After all, the birthday isn't till Wednesday."

"And by that time they'll be sold, all the maps will be sold," Susan cried wildly. "I expect thousands of trippers will be in the village this week-end and they'll all buy maps!"

"I don't see how they can if the shop's shut," said Midge reasonably.

They trailed disconsolately back to the little shop and tried to peer in at the high windows, past the bright-coloured china and earthenware.

"Give me a buckie-up, somebody, I can't see," said Susan.

Bill kindly bent down, and Susan scrambled on to his back. "Oh help," panted Bill, tottering, "this is more than I bargained for!"

Susan said, "Keep still, can't you. D'you know, I think there's somebody there. That showcase with the silver in it has been moved and I can see into the back-shop—I'm sure there's somebody— *Bill!*"

At that point Bill collapsed with Susan on top of him. Midge and Charlotte seemed to think that there was something funny about this. Bill picked himself up, groaning that his back was broken, and Susan ignored this in a very callous way and kept leaping into the air, trying to see in at the window and insisting that there was somebody inside.

"Well, let's knock and find out," said Midge.

"Good idea," said Susan, who didn't seem to have thought of this simple step. "Maybe Miss Frame is having a good tidy-out."

So they knocked loudly on the door. Nothing happened for a minute or two although Susan said she could hear someone moving about. "Knock again," said Susan. "Maybe she didn't hear."

"Knock yourself," said Midge. "If she can't hear that she must be dead."

So Susan knocked again, rather gingerly, and to their delight the door was unlocked and opened. It wasn't Miss Frame who stood there, but a dark young man who didn't look too pleased.

"Oh," said Susan, taken aback. "Is Miss Frame in?" she added.

"Miss Frame is away for the day," said the man. "Can I do anything for you?"

This must be the partner, they thought, who had started the side-line in maps.

"We're awfully sorry to bother you if the shop's shut," said Charlotte, "but we wanted to buy one of the maps. For a birthday present——"

"That's all right," said the man, "the shop is not really shut, I was busy and locked the door. Come in——"

Well, this was grand, they thought, and trooped in; but it was to be a day of disappointments. Aunt Lucy's map, they discovered, was twenty-five shillings, and they only had twenty-one and elevenpence.

"Wish we had got Miss Frame," Midge whispered unscrupulously, "she'd certainly have knocked off the odd three and a penny or whatever it is." However, the man showed absolutely no sign of being so accommodating, and they were obliged to take second best—one showing another part of the road. But this one had Farthing Green on it, which was nice too, they decided, and after all, as Charlotte said, Aunt Lucy wouldn't *know* that she might have had the other. The man wrapped it up, and they hid it in one of the pockets of the car, and went back to the Mill-House feeling pleased with themselves and quite ready for one of Mrs. Forester's sumptuous teas.

Apparently the cold weather had decided to reform, because when they woke on Easter Day, the sun was shining madly and the birds were singing madly too, and there were boiled eggs for breakfast, gaily-coloured, pink and green and yellow. There were other eggs too, Easter eggs— big chocolate ones from Dr. Carmichael, with chocolates inside; and cardboard ones decorated with rabbits and lambs and yellow chickens with presents inside from Aunt Lucy, and the little presents that they had given each other. Bill's presents, which he had been so secretive about, were pencils, carved and painted by himself— Susan's was all tiny flowers, and Midge's was a totem-pole. They were a tremendous hit, the only thing was, Susan said, that she couldn't possibly use hers as a *pencil* because she couldn't bear to sharpen it away.

After breakfast, Midge and Susan decided that there was just time before church to take Easter eggs round to Belle and the two children.

"And look here," said Cousin Barbara, "if you're going for a picnic this afternoon, do ask Belle and the children to join you. I'm sure they never have any fun and they don't seem to mix with any one in the village."

Everybody thought that this was a good idea.

Susan, who couldn't remember an Easter at home in Scotland when she and all her friends hadn't rolled hard-boiled eggs down the nearest hill on Easter Day, had been astonished to discover that this wasn't a universal custom. However, the Carmichaels, to her relief, had kept it up. "The only thing is," said Susan, "where are we going to find a hill in this flat landscape?"

"Oh, don't worry," said Midge, "we'll soon find a hill. After all, it doesn't need to be a mountain. I expect that Belle will know a nice gentle slope although I can't call one to mind myself at the moment."

Midge and Susan took the eggs round to Folly Cottage, while Charlotte and Bill did the washing-up. Aunt Lucy, who loved festivals, had decorated an old chip-basket raked out by Cousin Barbara with green and yellow tissue paper, and had arranged the three pretty eggs in it with three tiny fluffy yellow chicks perched on top. Belle and the two children seemed quite stunned.

"For *us*?" said Belle.

"For *us*?" whispered Mary, putting out a finger as if scarcely daring to touch the pretty basket. "I've never in my life had an Easter egg before!"

"For *us*? Oh, *thank* you!" said Robert, who was a very polite little boy.

Susan glanced at Belle, and saw to her horror that Belle's eyes were full of tears. Susan, who always joined in any tears that were going, knew that she would be howling herself in a minute. "There's something inside, you know," she gulped quickly. "Open them."

"Something inside as *well*?" said Mary incredulously. Rather shyly, she took her egg and opened it. Inside was a little wooden doll with black painted hair and jointed legs and arms and some gay frocks to dress it in. Robert had a dinky car, and inside Belle's egg was another tiny egg with a silver thimble in it—the Carmichaels had found this in an antique shop in Maidstone and were very proud of this present.

Belle was speechless. Robert flung himself on the floor and began zooming happily round chairs and table legs. Susan in her helpful way showed Mary how to put the doll's clothes on and how easy it was to cut out more from old scraps of cloth. Midge said, "Oh, and will you please all come for a picnic with us this afternoon?"

Instantly all Belle's old reserve came back. She frowned and put on what Susan called her "you can't do anything for me" face, and was just beginning to say abruptly, "Oh, no thanks——" when a clamour broke out from Mary and Robert.

"Oh Belle, we must, we must——!"

"Please, Belle, *please* say yes——"

"Belle, let us! You must let us!"

Midge said, when she could make herself heard, "There you are, Belle. Carried *nem con*—whatever that may mean."

"It means *nemine contradicente*, no one objecting, actually," said Susan officiously, as if anybody cared.

"Oh well, there's one objecting," said Midge, "but you'll have to give way, Belle, really you will, because you can see that the kids want to go, and as a matter of fact we need you to find us a hill we can roll our eggs down."

"Are we going to roll eggs down a hill?" said Robert.

"Not our pretty ones!" said Mary, alarmed.

"No, no, hard-boiled ones," said Susan. "And then you eat them. It's an old Scottish custom. At least it may be a custom other places as well for all I know, but we always used to do it at home."

"All right then," said Midge, "we'll call round for you about two. And we'd better push off now, Susie, or we'll be late for church."

Belle gave a shriek. "So will we!" she cried, and in the ensuing bustle said no more against going to the picnic.

"You know," said Midge, as they cycled back to the farm, "I hate to admit it, Susie, but I'm beginning to think you're right and that there *is* a mystery about that family. How could that kid never have had an Easter egg before?"

"Well, I suppose it's *possible* never to have had an Easter egg," said Susan doubtfully. "Some people may not bother about Easter eggs. I love Easter almost as much as Christmas, only there's not so much of it——"

"Yes, well, never mind that," said Midge. "The

thing is, I do believe that there is a mystery about them."

"I'm certain there is," said Susan. "I'd better start investigating into their past again. Tactfully, of course."

"Oh help!" said Midge.

It was when they were opening the gate of Folly Cottage that afternoon to call for Belle and the children, that Susan suddenly said, "Oh, jings, I've just remembered what that photo in Mrs. Forester's album reminded me of—the photo of Belle's mother! I didn't notice it this morning or I'd have thought of it sooner. I must have another squint at it."

But when she pushed her way into the cottage, which really wasn't necessary because all three were waiting on the doorstep, the photograph was gone.

"Where's the photo of your mother gone, Belle?" she said.

Belle looked up from a bustle about Mary's Wellingtons and Robert's mack and scowled. "I put it away," she said. "The glass is broken."

Mary, having decided to put on boots, was on the floor taking off her shoes. "No, it isn't, Belle," she said. "I saw the photo in the drawer upstairs and the glass was all right."

Susan, her face pink with excitement, opened her mouth to speak when Midge kicked her, savagely but unobtrusively, on the ankle. Susan glared at her indignantly, but Midge frowned at Susan and slightly shook her head.

"Well, come on then," said Midge, "if we're all ready."

Belle locked the door and hid the key under a stone, and the party moved off. Robert attached himself to Bill with dog-like devotion. Midge and Susan lagged behind a little.

Susan could hardly speak for excitement. "There, there, there you are, Midge!" she stammered. "That's suspicious if you like! I'd never have given the photo another thought if she hadn't gone and hidden it! Oh, Midge, *do* you think they're Mrs. Forester's long-lost nieces?"

"Well, Robert isn't," said Midge fatuously.

"Oh, *Midge*, don't be an ass," said Susan impatiently. "I'm sure they are."

"Much as I'd like to think so," said Midge, "I doubt it. Too much of a coincidence."

"But coincidences *do* happen," said Susan. "You wouldn't believe the coincidences that are happening to Mummy in Africa!"

"Yes, they do, I know," said Midge. "And I think that Mrs. Forester's relations could just as easily turn up the middle of Kent as in the middle of anywhere else. But in that case, what I can't understand is Belle's attitude. Belle's trying to *hide* something. She must know by now who Mrs. Forester is after hearing everybody talking about her—why, she was in the room when Cousin Barbara first mentioned Evelyn Gardiner!"

"Yes, and she got such a turn that she dropped the logs!" said Susan eagerly. "I never connected it before, but that's what happened! And she listened at the door!"

"But Susie," said Midge, "if Mrs. Forester is Belle's aunt, then Belle must *know* that she's her aunt, right?"

Susan nodded.

"Then why didn't she go rushing to her with open arms as soon as she heard that she was in the district?"

"Because of the old quarrel?" Susan suggested.

"We-e-el, maybe," said Midge. "Belle *may* bear grudges, but if I was in her place I'd rather have a live aunt than an old dead quarrel——"

"Ugh, me too," Susan agreed.

"But now I come to think of it," Midge went on slowly, "Belle goes out of her way to avoid Mrs. Forester. I know that she never usually waits at the farm after lunch, but that day Mrs. Forester was coming to tea, she was in a mighty hurry to be off—don't you remember, I had to wash the beastly dishes? It didn't strike me at the time, but now it does. Besides, there's no indication that she's lost an aunt. She's *got* this aunt she mentioned—in London or wherever she is."

"Ugh, yes," said Susan, with deep disappointment. "All the same," she said, cheering up again, "there's *something* queer about Belle. Even avoiding Mrs. Forester is queer. I'm sure she's hiding something."

"Yes," said Midge, "and you're not likely to find out what it is by questioning her. You've been snooping round her ever since she came back, and you haven't found out a single thing. You've only put her on her guard——"

"I suppose that's why you kicked me," said Susan humbly.

"Of course," said Midge. "Now, if we tried pumping the younger ones——"

Susan gazed with admiration at her astute cousin.

"Come on," said Midge, "or we'll get left behind."

Belle led the party across a field and into the little wood which looked over to Folly Cottage on the far side of which lay a gentle slope that she knew of. Bill and Robert went off on some manly pursuit connected with catching a rabbit; Charlotte and Belle were ahead. Everywhere the wood was bright with clumps of primroses and violets, and starry with anemones.

Mary danced about, exclaiming, "Oh, aren't they lovely! Oh, they're so lovely! Midge, what are they called?"

"They're anemones," said Midge, surprised at her not knowing. "Their other name is wind-flowers. But I shouldn't pick them if I were you —they droop at once."

"Wind-flowers! That's a nice name," said Mary. "And I certainly shan't pick them. I like them growing."

Midge said, "Weren't you brought up in the country then, Mary?"

"Oh yes," said Mary, "sort of. But African country isn't like English country."

Susan's fingers dug into Midge's arm.

"Mary——" began Susan.

"Mary!" Belle's voice called from farther along

the path and Belle came back to meet them. "Oh, there you are, Mary," she said, scowling a little when she saw the three together, "I thought you were lost," she said; and from that minute until the picnic was over did not leave Mary alone with Susan and Midge again.

CHAPTER SEVEN

BONFIRE

AT LUNCH-TIME on Easter Monday Cousin Barbara said, "I'm sorry really that you're thinking of a visit to Canterbury to-day, for it would have been a good idea to have a bonfire down in the wood."

"A bonfire!" cried Midge.

"Ugh, a bonfire would be great!" said Susan.

"Who wants to go to boring old Canterbury anyway?" said Bill. "A bonfire would be much more fun."

"Well——" said Dr. Carmichael.

"We could take potatoes down and roast them in the ashes," said Cousin Barabara cunningly.

That settled it, of course. Canterbury hadn't a chance against potatoes roasted in the ashes of a bonfire.

"Oh goodness," cried Aunt Lucy. "I haven't eaten potatoes roasted in a fire for quite twenty years! I'm afraid they won't taste so good now as they did then. And even then I seem to remember that there was always a nasty hard little raw lump in the middle——"

"Nonsense, Lucy," said Dr. Carmichael, "they were delicious."

"You can't have done them properly," said Cousin Barbara. "Come along then, let's all hurry with the dishes. Belle, you and the children will come with us, of course—you'd like to, wouldn't you? Oh, good——"

It was a dry day, with blinks of sun, but with a cold north-east wind blowing; just right, Cousin Barbara declared, for a bonfire—and there would be no lack of fuel, for there were always bits of the wood that wanted clearing. The more responsible members of the party armed themselves with bill-hooks, Robert carried a basket of potatoes, Belle had been entrusted with a bottle of paraffin to get the fire going.

In the wood they had very little time to-day for the clumps of primroses and the distant deep-blue glimmer of the first bluebells. Cousin Barbara led the way along a little path to a clearing in the tangled undergrowth and directed operations from there. The children brought dry branches to start the fire and the grown-ups hacked down great piles of dog-roses and brambles and suckers of all kinds as fuel. Cousin Barbara and Dr. Carmichael worked like blacks; Aunt Lucy did too, really, but she was inclined to be fidgety on account of the bill-hooks, for whenever a grown-up laid one down to draw breath, it was seized on by Robert or Bill, and though Aunt Lucy didn't mind their hacking at the undergrowth, she felt convinced that they would soon be hacking at their toes. Susan and Mary spent most of their time agitating for the fire to be started, but this Cousin Barbara wouldn't allow until there was a really sufficient pile of fuel in readiness to keep it going. Midge occasionally

appeared with a rather small twig which she laid
tenderly on the pile, and then disappeared again
for another long interval. Charlotte, manfully
dragging what felt like whole trees to the clearing,
suspected a book in her coat pocket but never
actually caught her at it.

Belle, conscientious as always, was tackling all
the really vicious-looking rose canes. She looked
happy and animated for once, and not so sulky
as usual, Susan thought, coming over to talk to
her. She noticed round her neck what looked like
a ring on a thin gold chain, tossed out from under
her jumper by her exertions. "So that's what is
on the end of that chain," thought Susan, "I
wondered—— What's that you wear, Belle?"
she asked, pointing to it, when Belle stopped to
take a breath.

"Oh that?" said Belle. She hastily thrust it back
under her jumper and scowled. "That's my
mother's engagement ring," she mumbled. "I
wear it underneath."

"Jings," thought Susan, "I'd like to have a keek
at that sometime, but I suppose I'd have to knock
her senseless first——"

"Well, all you people," called Cousin Barbara,
"I should think we might start it now—what
d'you think, Charles?"

Uncle Charles agreed fervently; Cousin Barbara
arranged a good pile of dry kindling and sprinkled
it with paraffin; Uncle Charles put a match to it
and the flames leapt up. Soon the dry branches
were crackling merrily. "When it really gets
going," said Cousin Barbara, "it will burn any-

thing, but feed it only with dry wood just now——"

"What about the potatoes?" said Susan. "I'm getting jolly hungry."

"Not just yet," said Uncle Charles. "When we get a really good heart to the fire we'll put in the potatoes."

Stoking the bonfire was much more fun than gathering sticks and fuel for it, the children thought as they flung on the branches. The wind came with sudden gusts and sent flames and smoke towards them as they leapt laughing out of the way; their eyes were sore with the sharp sting of the smoke and smuts fell on their clothes and hair. "Now we'll put the potatoes in," said Cousin Barbara, and dropped the potatoes into the glowing heart of the fire.

Susan expected them to be ready in about five minutes. Cousin Barbara and Uncle Charles laughed at her. "They're not nearly ready," said Cousin Barbara.

"Gracious, no," Aunt Lucy agreed. "I can remember waiting for what must have been *hours* for the potatoes to be ready."

"And don't stand about there doing nothing," called Uncle Charles. "Get more fuel! Look, all that pile we cut has nearly gone!" He threw a huge rose-bush on the fire and the flames caught the wicked-looking thorns and set the new young leaves blazing.

"It seems a shame to burn them," said Cousin Barbara, "for the wild roses look so pretty in the summer. But we *must* clear the wood a little."

They all bustled about getting more stuff to burn, and then at last Cousin Barbara thought the potatoes would be ready. She poked them out of the fire with a long stick. "Oh, just a minute, Susie!" she cried. "They're burning hot, let them cool a little!"

"But it's half the fun, surely," said Charlotte, "to get your fingers burnt——" and she seized the charred object which didn't look as if there was an edible bite in it, and broke it in two and began to eat the delicious, floury inside. Cousin Barbara came in for much praise for her excellent timing, the potatoes were cooked to perfection.

"I was quite wrong you know," said Aunt Lucy dreamily. "They taste just as wonderful as ever they did—better than you would think it possible for a potato to taste. And somehow, that occasional bite of burnt, ashy skin only adds to the flavour!"

"This is much better than Canterbury," said Bill, starting on his third, "and I vote that we have a bonfire every day."

CHAPTER EIGHT

A LUCKY ENCOUNTER

THAT EVENING Dr. Carmichael went back to London; and on Tuesday morning Susan decided that the time for play was over and that she must immediately concentrate on unravelling the mystery of Belle. While Midge was still blissfully sleeping in her little bed, Susan, washed and dressed, took out a pencil and paper and began to write down her findings in orderly fashion. She wrote in large capitals:

POINTS IN COMMON BETWEEN BELLE'S FAMILY AND MISSING FAMILY

BELLE'S FAMILY	MISSING FAMILY
(1) Been in Africa.	(1) Brought up in Africa.
(2) Ages: 16: 9: 7.	(2) Ages: 16: 9: 7.
(3) Names: Belle, Mary, Robert.	(3) Evelyn, Mary, Robert.

N.B.—Two out of three names the same.
Objection.—Mary, Robert, very common names.
Query.—Could Belle be a pet-name for Evelyn?

N.B.—I said from the beginning that Belle wasn't Belle's real name. At this point in her notes Susan suddenly exclaimed to herself, "What an *idiot* I am! What about their surname I never even thought of asking! That would settle the whole thing!" Then she thought, "Or would it? Supposing Belle is using a false name? But would she dare to do that? Wouldn't it be awkward? Even if *she* always remembered what her name was supposed to be, the kids never would. I know *I* never would. I'd be always giving the show away. Belle can tell lies like anything, but she could hardly rely on the kids doing that—look how Mary came straight out with that about the photograph and about living in Africa—I mean Belle *knows* that Mary can't be relied on not to pop everything out—that's why she won't let me talk to her alone. So I shouldn't think she'd risk changing their name."

At this point she darted to Midge's bed and began shaking her. After a lot of effort on Susan's part Midge opened one eye and grunted.

"Ugh, *Midge!*" Susan begged. "Do wake up!"

"What *is* it?" Midge muttered crossly.

"Midge, are you listening? Midge, what's Belle's other name?" said Susan.

Midge opened both eyes and glared rather venomously at Susan. "D'you mean to say," she said, "that you woke me up in the middle of the night to ask me Belle's name?"

"Yes, of course," said Susan. "It's important. Besides, it's seven o'clock."

"That's what I said," said Midge, "the middle of the night. And anyway, how should I know what her name is?" She turned away and hunched the blankets round her shoulder. "Good night," she said firmly.

"Oh, *Midge*," said Susan in disgust. "Well, did you happen to hear the name of Mrs. Forester's nieces?"

"Smith," came an indistinct mumble from the bed-clothes.

Susan was so enraged that she jumped off her bed in order to stamp her foot. "*Smith!*" she exclaimed. "Smith, of all names! Why did it have to be Smith? Why couldn't it be—be—Montmorency or something? Something un-usual?"

"Susie," murmured Midge plaintively, "I do wish you'd shut up and let me go to sleep."

"You lazy big tumphy," said Susan. But now that she had the idea of finding out Belle's name, she wasn't going to be thwarted. She went downstairs to look for Cousin Barbara, whom she knew to be an early riser. She found her cleaning the fireplace in the sitting-room.

"Hallo, Susan," said Cousin Barbara, "you're on the move early, aren't you?"

"Oh, I like getting up early—sometimes," said Susan. "Cousin Barbara," she went on, "what's Belle's other name?"

"Her surname you mean?" said Cousin Barbara. "Smith."

Susan nearly fainted with astonishment. "Smith!" she exclaimed. "Well, I never! Smith!"

"That surprises you, does it?" said Cousin Barbara, grinning at her. "I'm sure you thought that Belle was a princess in disguise. You've been trailing round at her heels for days trying to pump her, haven't you?"

"But Cousin Barbara," said Susan, not wanting to say too much, "don't *you* think there's something mysterious about Belle?"

"Well," said Cousin Barbara, "she's extremely reticent about herself and her past. *I* couldn't get any more out of her than you could—I gave up trying after a while. And it's a little surprising to find her doing my housework. I should have expected her to be still at school or preparing for a career instead of working for her living doing my chores."

"That's what *I* said," said Susan triumphantly, "but Midge or Charlotte or somebody said that you couldn't tell these hard times, because all sorts of people did all sorts of things."

"Yes, that's true enough," Cousin Barbara agreed. "And one certain thing is that Belle wants to be left alone and not bothered——"

"Ugh, *I'm* not going to bother her, Cousin Barabara," said Susan. No fear, she thought, because she could get much more information from Mary!

Now that she was up and about, Susan felt that she had better offer to help, so Cousin Barbara set her to laying the table and making toast, and the others came down to find her glowing with conscious virtue.

That morning they decided to cycle into Folding, for Bill had found a shilling that had slipped into the lining of his coat and wanted to spend it.

They were on their way home—they had passed the pretty silver birch thicket, and the derelict water-mill and they had just turned the corner into the straight stretch of road that ran along by the river and were admiring the catkins like lambs' tails, when Bill said sharply, "What are these two men doing?" and pointed to two men in the distance just before the road turned away from the river.

"They're throwing stones at something," said Midge.

"Surely," said Bill, beginning to pedal hard, "*surely* they couldn't be throwing stones at the swans! That's just where the nest is! Oh, the *fiends*!" He pedalled furiously.

With expressions of rage and disgust, the girls followed. They had no idea what Bill meant to do, and were rather alarmed to see him charge straight at the men on his bicycle.

"Bill, *don't*!" called Charlotte sharply, but it was too late—one of the louts seized Bill's handle-bars and roughly thrust them sideways. Bill and the bicycle went sprawling.

"How *dare* you, how *dare* you!" shouted Charlotte.

"Leave that little boy alone!" yelled Midge.

"Come on," cried Susan, "charge!"

The sight of three avenging females—on bicycles—advancing on them was too much for the men. They hesitated only a second, then turned and fled to a lorry which was parked a little way along the road. They climbed in and immediately drove away.

The girls dismounted and hurried to the aid of Bill, who, unhurt except for grazed knees and hands, was struggling to his feet. "Oh, I'm all right, thanks," he replied to their inquiries. "And the poor swan seems all right——"

"Sitting there on her nest as if nothing had happened," said Midge in amazement, "looking quite unperturbed!"

"Could you imagine any people being such *brutes*?" said Charlotte indignantly. "Stopping their beastly lorry just to throw stones at a poor defenceless swan! And they weren't just loutish boys either, one of them was a grown-up man!"

"Is your bike all right, Bill?" said Susan.

When Bill was examining his bicycle which, fortunately, was not damaged, another person appeared on the scene, a small, rather tubby, well-scrubbed looking man with a bristly moustache, wearing tweeds and with a spaniel at his heels. He approached them across the field at the other side of the road.

"Well done! Well done!" he shouted as he came. "Scoundrels! Scoundrels! Saw it all as I came across the field. Like to put *them* in a nest and throw stones at them. Pity we ever got rid of the stocks. Just the thing for hooligans. Are you hurt, boy?"

"Oh no, thank you sir," Bill assured him. "Just a graze. It'll be perfectly all right when I wash it."

By this time the little man had come through the gate and was examining Bill's injuries. "H'm. Dirty," he said. "Very dirty. Wants a good wash

in disinfectant immediately. Where you staying,
eh? Strangers in these parts, aren't you?"

Charlotte explained that they were staying with
their cousin at Apple-tree Farm.

"Apple-tree Farm! These new-fangled names!
Always been known as Hubble's as long as *I* can
remember. And hundreds of years before that.
Mrs. Trent has it now—she's your cousin, eh?
Well, too far away. Folding's only a step. Come
with me and get it cleaned up."

Susan and the Carmichaels glanced at each
other. Folding! This must be Sir Hubert himself!
They collected their bicycles and retraced their
steps.

"How strange that Apple-tree Farm should have
belonged to people called Hubble!" said Charlotte,
making conversation. "There was a Hubble had
one of the earliest kilns for firing earthenware at
Wrotham, and that isn't far from here!   I
wonder——"

"Hubble is a common name in this part of
Kent," said Sir Hubert. "There have been Hubbles
in the farms as long as there have been Foldings
in the Manor. Longer, perhaps. You like these
china knick-knacks? Get my sister to show you
her collection of Chelsea toys—scent-bottles,
thimbles, seals—nonsense like that, but pretty.
Don't make things like that these days."

Sir Hubert led them by a short-cut through the
silver birch grove, through the gardens enclosed
by the wonderful old yew hedges and into the
house. Bill, who had a very taking way with
him, sympathised with Sir Hubert about the loss

of the Folding Letter, and inquired if anything had been heard of it. Sir Hubert, whose abrupt manner obviously hid a kind heart, summoned the ancient housekeeper to fetch boiled water and cotton-wool and disinfectant and cleaned up Bill's wounds with his own hands. "No, not a word about the Letter. Scoundrels! Scoundrels! Fine thing when you can't have an old letter in your house but some snivelling collector comes and helps himself. Don't know what the country's coming to. Scoundrels! Funny thing to steal, if you ask me. Perfectly good Constable hanging on the wall. Lovely little picture, rather look at it than an old letter any day of the week——" He was clearly a little insulted that his lovely Constable had been passed over in favour of an old letter, even if Shakespeare did write it.

Finally, nothing more could be done for Bill; cake and lemonade—fizzy too—was produced for the whole party, and Sir Hubert showed them to the gate. Just as they were leaving, he thrust something into Bill's hand.

"Oh, no thank you, sir, really," Bill demurred, going a bit pink round the ears.

"Come along now," barked Sir Hubert, "don't refuse an old man. Always something boys and girls can do with a tip. Share it, share it."

"Well, thank you, sir," said Bill. "Very sporting of you, sir."

"Very sporting of *you*, my boy. Tackling two great louts——"

And with mutual expressions of esteem, they parted.

"Well, blow me down!" exclaimed Bill as they wheeled their bicycles down the drive. "Two pounds!"

"Two pounds!" cried Midge and Charlotte.

"*Two pounds!*" cried Susan. "Just because you did that! He must be rolling in money."

"People who are rolling in money don't always give it away," said Bill.

"Oh, I agree," said Susan. "The more they're rolling the more they're inclined to stick to it, if you ask me."

"The dear kind fellow," said Midge.

"Two pounds!" said Bill again. "I say," he said slowly, "we could get that other map for Aunt Lucy now! And *still* have something over for ourselves. If you girls agree——"

Of course they agreed. They were quite pleased with the map which they had got, but to be able to give Aunt Lucy another one, and one which she specially wanted—well, that would be a splendid start to any collection, they felt.

"Oh, come on then," said Susan, eager as ever, "let's go now in case it's sold."

"Is it too late to cycle this morning?" said Midge.

"No, no," said Charlotte, "it's only about six miles to Farthing Green from here, and it can't be more than eleven o'clock now—we can easily do it by lunch-time."

"Thank goodness that we don't have to walk," said Midge.

CHAPTER NINE

CURIOUS BEHAVIOUR OF AN ANTIQUE DEALER

THERE WAS no hitch this time. The shop was open and Miss Frame was in attendance. But a really terrifying hitch appeared when Miss Frame couldn't find the map they wanted. They described it to her, and she said yes, yes, she knew exactly the one they meant, and she hunted through the framed maps which were on a chair, and she couldn't find it anywhere. Susan and the Carmichaels could hardly believe their ears, and Miss Frame was as distressed as they were.

"Oh dear!" she said, her little pink and white face all woebegone. "It *is* so disappointing for you! I wonder," she said, "I wonder if by *any* chance Mr. Smith has put it in the back where he does all his framing."

Another Smith! Susan thought to herself as they crowded after Miss Frame into the tiny room behind the shop. "If I really had an inflamed imagination or spring fever, as Charlotte says, I'd be making something of that——"

There was a sudden cry of delight from Miss Frame. "Here it is! That's the one, isn't it? Oh, but I wonder," she added doubtfully, "I wonder if Mr. Smith has put it aside for a customer?"

This was too much. They set to work on Miss Frame, and eventually convinced her that as the map had no name on it, no ticket on it even, then it wasn't being kept for any one. She wrapped it up for them in a rather untidy piece of brown paper, and they went off rejoicing.

There were two bicycles propped up against Miss Frame's cottage. Susan assumed that they belonged to Miss Frame and Mr. Smith and stopped to examine the tyres of the nearest one. She became quite excited when she saw that the tyres matched the diagram that they had drawn at Folding Manor. So did Bill, until he noticed that the other bicycle had the same tyres and that both were of a make which was practically a household word.

"Bang goes our Clue!" he said disgustedly.

They hurried after Midge and Charlotte, and found them talking to Mrs. Forester by the bridge at the end of the lane leading to the Mill-House. She was intrigued to hear of their errand, and they unwrapped the map and showed it to her.

Charlotte looked at it with her head on one side. "D'you know," she said, "I don't think that frame suits it——"

Susan cried out in protest, but Mrs. Forester said, "Why, Charlotte, I was thinking just that very same thing, only I didn't want to say anything to spoil it for you. I thought myself that it wasn't quite Mr. Smith's usual good taste."

"I think that both maps we've got would look better if we swopped their frames," said Bill. "I'll see what I can do when we get home. If it doesn't look nice, we'll take it back after Aunt Lucy's birthday and get Mr. Smith to change the frame."

The others agreed that this would be best, and they were about to take their leave of Mrs. Forester when Susan, who never liked to miss an opportunity, said, "No news about the nieces. I suppose, Mrs. Forester?"

"Oh Susan!" cried Mrs. Forester, and it suddenly dawned on them that she was looking quite drawn and ill. "There is news, but such bad and worrying news! I had word from my lawyer this morning. He has contacted the African lawyers and they write to say that the children came back to England to join their aunt, Miss Evelyn Gardiner!"

There was a stunned silence.

"But that's you!" cried Susan at last. "But what does it *mean*? Does it mean that they've been kidnapped or what?"

"Oh, I don't know what it means," said Mrs. Forester unhappily. "Eight months since they came to England!"

"But who could have kidnapped them?" said Charlotte. "And why?"

"Well, they're rather rich, you know," said Mrs. Forester.

"Rich?" said Susan. "I thought that their father was a farmer and that they were very poor?"

"Yes, but they inherited their mother's money that she wasn't allowed to spend, I suppose, and Great-aunt Amanda left half her money to me and half to my sister, and she was *very* rich. But even so," said Mrs. Forester, "I guess it wasn't enough to tempt kidnappers. No, there has been some terrible mistake somewhere. On Thursday morning I have an appointment with the lawyer who saw the children in London, I fixed it by telephone this morning. The tiresome man couldn't see me sooner, he said. In fact, he seemed to think he was doing me a favour seeing me so soon, so I guess I'll just have to be patient. To-morrow, of course, I'm coming over to Apple-tree Farm for your aunt's birthday tea, and I'll tell you more about it then."

The Carmichaels and Susan bade her good-bye and cycled off. They discussed this perfectly in-comprehensible development in the story of Mrs. Forester's nieces; and even Susan, inflamed imagination and all, couldn't offer an explanation. She signalled to Midge to lag behind a little.

"How would this fit in with Belle?" she said.

"Not at all," said Midge emphatically. "Would *you* do Cousin Barbara's housework if you were rolling in money?"

"Oh help, no," said Susan. "But maybe the kidnappers have stolen all the money by this time?"

"Well, maybe they have," said Midge slowly after thought. "But if so, what d'you imagine Belle was doing all the time? I shouldn't call her a weak character—I can't visualise Belle sitting around doing nothing while somebody steals her money. And she'd be an absolute tiger if some-body tried to steal the kids' money."

"But what could she do?" said Susan.

"Well, surely," said Midge, "she could go to the lawyers, or the police. This is England, after all, and she's not in durance vile."

"No," said Susan, "she isn't. And I can't imagine any kidnappers stealing her money and then letting her loose to tell her story to any Tom, Dick or Harry who came along."

"You're right," Midge agreed. "But on the other hand, she hasn't exactly shown any inclination to tell *us* her story, has she? Far less Tom, Dick and Harry."

"It's like getting blood out of a stone," said Susan regretfully.

"Well, there you are," said Midge.

"Where am I?" said Susan.

"As Belle isn't in the clutches of kidnappers, then Belle isn't Mrs. Forester's long-lost niece," Midge explained.

"But," Susan objected, "we don't *know* that Mrs. Forester's nieces are in the clutches of kidnappers either. And I must say, Midge, I think that there are far too many coincidences for Belle and the kids *not* to be Mrs. Forester's long-lost nieces—and nephew. If you see what I mean," she added, getting a bit muddled herself now. "I mean, they're both called Smith, for one thing."

"*Are* they?" said Midge, surprised.

"Oh, of course, I forgot that you were asleep when Cousin Barbara told me," said Susan.

"Well, but Susie," said Midge, "*Smith* of all names! There must be *millions* of Mary Smiths and Robert Smiths and even Belle Smiths!"

"Yes," said Susan, "but not millions of Mary, Robert and Belle Smiths all in one lot."

"In the case of Mrs. Forester's lot, it's Mary, Robert and Evelyn Smith," said Midge.

"But don't you think," said Susan, "that Belle might have changed her name? As a sort of disguise?"

"Why not change the others' names too, then?" said Midge. "And change their surname?"

"Who'd bother to change the name of Smith? I mean, it's like an assumed name anyway. And Midge," cried Susan, getting excited again, "the other two are so young! Could she risk it, d'you think? She'd be bound to think that they'd forget and give the show away! And you know that I said from the beginning that I was sure 'Belle' wasn't her real name!"

"Oh, I know you said that," said Midge, "but then you say some perfectly foolish things."

"Sometimes they're not potty," said Susan.

"No," agreed Midge, beginning to waver a little. "I must say you do come away with a sort of inspired guess sometimes."

"Inspired guess!" said Susan indignantly. "Masterly pieces of deduction!"

"Yes, well, we needn't argue about that," said Midge. "The thing is, we must get more evidence. And our only hope is Mary, or possibly Robert. We'll try and get her alone. They're over at the farm every day since Cousin Barbara told Belle that she must bring them with her when the school is on holiday and not leave them alone at the cottage."

"We'll tackle her to-morrow then," said Susan.

"Now look, pet," said Midge, "this is where we want to be tactful and go carefully. We don't want you blundering in upsetting the infant, because if Belle realises what we're up to, I shouldn't put it past her to fold up her tent like the Arabs and silently steal away."

"I'll leave it all to you," Susan said handsomely, and, at that moment, she really meant it. "Wouldn't it be too heavenly and wonderful and marvellous if we could present Mrs. Forester with her long-lost nieces—and nephew—when she comes to tea to-morrow?" And Susan went into a blissful daze at the very thought; to the great danger of anyone who happened to be cycling with her.

"Oh Susie, you owl, look *out!*" Midge shouted. "You nearly had me in the ditch then. And now look at you, on the wrong side of the road! If a car had come round the corner then, you would have been under it! And I must say," she added, "if it will calm you down at all, I've never seen a long-lost niece less anxious to be presented than Belle."

"Midge!" Susan was suddenly struck with a terrible idea. "You don't think that Belle could be the Mad Collector, do you? And that is the secret that she's trying to hide?"

"'Course not, stupid," said Midge, "she hasn't got a bicycle."

Susan giggled. Then she sobered and said sadly, "I *wish* you would take me seriously, Midge!"

At lunch-time they recounted their morning's adventures—all except the buying of the map, of course—to Aunt Lucy and Cousin Barbara; and after lunch they went upstairs to Bill's room to see what he proposed to do about changing the frames.

"Definitely the maps would look nicer if the frames were changed," said Charlotte, who as quite a talented drawer herself was looked on as the art expert of the family, "but Bill, can you do it?"

"Of course," said Bill. "It's only a matter of removing that backing of sticky paper; and I have a roll of sticky paper so that I can do the maps up again."

Susan was amazed at Bill's practical mind; Charlotte and Midge were used to it. Susan gazed at him with admiration as he stripped the paper off the back of the frame and carefully removed the glass and the map and the backing. Then he started on the other one, and Susan, in her helpful way, successfully managed to disarrange the whole thing, so that a dirty piece of paper stuck out about half an inch from between the map and the carboard backing. Susan pulled it out a little.

"Oh Susie, you ass," said Bill, without heat "you couldn't just leave the thing alone, could you, till I'm ready for it?"

"But what's this bit of paper *for*, Bill?" said Susan.

"I expect it's an extra bit of backing," said Bill absently, at work on the other frame.

Susan gently pulled the paper out from between the map and the cardboard backing and turned it over. "But Bill," she said, "it has funny sort of writing on it."

"Some old piece of paper he's using up," said Bill.

"But Bill," said Susan again, "*look* at it! It's a letter or something."

Bill and Charlotte looked up then. Midge, who was lying on Bill's bed reading a book, came across the room and looked over Susan's shoulder. Nobody said anything at all. They gazed at the dirty little piece of paper in Susan's hands and they said nothing. And then Charlotte stretched out a trembling finger and pointed to the crabbed signature.

"*W. Shakespeare,*" she breathed.

"Shakespeare?" repeated Bill stupidly.

"Shakespeare?" said Midge. "Have we found another Shakespeare letter, then?"

"Not another one," said Charlotte slowly.

Susan suddenly came to life. "Shakespeare! You don't mean that this scruffy little bit of paper is the Folding Letter?"

"I—I think it must be," said Charlotte.

"Is that what all the fuss was about?" said Bill. He dug into his pocket and after producing a lot of useful articles like nails and a compass and bits of string, he found the dirty, screwed-up piece of paper that he was looking for. "I've got the size written down here somewhere," he said. "Yes, here it is—$6\frac{1}{2}$ by 4—yes, that's $6\frac{1}{2}$ by 4 I should say, but what an awful-looking bit of paper!"

"But Bill!" said Charlotte, still overcome by awe. "Shakespeare *wrote* it! Touched that piece of paper or parchment or whatever it is and wrote on it!"

They all pondered this for a little and were certainly very impressed, all except Bill. "He wasn't a very good writer," he said with fellow-feeling.

"You don't understand," said Charlotte, who seemed to know more about Shakespeare than the others expected, "they wrote differently in those days—they used what is now called the old English script, quite different from our writing——"

"How do *you* know?" said Midge.

"I read it in *The Times* when the *Letter* was stolen," Charlotte confessed.

"Even so," said Bill, "I still think it's a very disappointing paper to be having such a fuss made of it."

"But how did it get into Aunt Lucy's map?" said Susan.

"I suppose the Mad Collector put it there," said Midge.

Susan gave a little shriek. While certainly enthralled with accounts of the Mad Collector's exploits and eager as she was to be mixed up with any sort of excitement, she hadn't quite bargained for coming to such close quarters with him as this.

"But does that mean, then," said Charlotte slowly, "that Miss Frame is the Mad Collector?"

"That little dainty Dresden shepherdess!" gasped Susan. "Oh, surely not!"

The others began to giggle rather hysterically.

"Well, after all," gasped Midge eventually, "she has a bicycle!"

This set them off again, all except Susan, who was protesting indignantly, "Really!" she said. "How you can say such a thing! That sweet old lady! And having such a struggle to keep her dear wee shop going!"

"Well!" shrieked Charlotte, wiping her eyes, "it'll be easier to keep her wee shop going if she dabbles in burglary as a sideline!"

Susan said furiously, "How *can* you talk in that heartless way?"

It wasn't often that the sweet-tempered Susan raged at them. Her cousins sobered down eventually.

"Oh Susie, I *do* agree," cried Charlotte. "It's no laughing matter. Miss Frame a thief!"

"I wasn't really laughing at poor Miss Frame," said Midge. "It was just at the idea of a Dresden shepherdess being a burglar in her spare time."

"But look here, you clots," said Bill, "Miss Frame can't have put the Folding Letter in the map——"

"Why not?" said Susan eagerly.

"Well, because she wouldn't have sold it to us for twenty-five shillings if she'd put it there!"

"Oh, of course not! Oh, thank *goodness*!" cried Susan. "But then, who did? What about the partner?"

"The partner, yes! He has a bike too!"

"Yes, but all the same," said Midge reluctantly. "I hate to say it, but Miss Frame must be mixed up with it, I should think."

"I don't believe it," said Susan. "And listen,

what's the idea of putting the Letter behind an old map anyway?"

"Well," said Charlotte, "I don't know, of course, but maybe we've discovered how the Mad Collector manages to get rid of the stolen manuscripts—you know that bit in the papers said that it had never been discovered what became of the stolen things, or how they were smuggled out of the country? Well, perhaps this is how they're smuggled out— hidden behind an old map. The Mad Collector steals them, hides them behind something of not much value, and an innocent-looking old map is carried off to France or America or any- where!"

"Goodness," said Bill, "maybe you're right, Charlotte! Won't Mr. Bristow be pleased?"

"You're not going to tell Mr. Bristow?" cried Susan.

"Sure," said Bill. "You wanted to help him, didn't you?"

"But what about Miss Frame?" wailed Susan. "Oh Bill, wait——!"

"If she's innocent, she'll be all right," said Midge. "And if she isn't, then she jolly well *ought* to be locked up, nice wee shop or no nice wee shop."

"But here's another thing," said Susan, "what about the reward? We might not get it with only the Folding Letter. The paper mentioned the other manuscripts as well."

"Golly, I'd forgotten the reward," said Bill.

"Don't you think it would be better," said Susan, "to do a bit of investigating on our own account? Once we've told the police *we* won't be allowed to help——"

"And a very good thing, too," said Charlotte, "*I* don't want to be mixed up in anything criminal."

"We won't be, silly," said Susan. "But you must admit that it would be much more exciting if we could catch the Mad Collector and find the other manuscripts and hand the whole lot over to Mr. Bristow and spite that la-di-da sergeant from Folding and get the reward and prove Miss Frame's innocence into the bargain!"

"Catch the Mad Collector!" said Charlotte faintly, but nobody paid any attention to her. Bill was quite carried away by the idea of capturing the Mad Collector by their own un-aided efforts, and even Midge didn't see what possible harm it could do to wait a *little* while before telling Mr. Bristow what had happened. "He'll get the glory in the end," she said. "And in the meantime we might as well be doing a spot of detection on our own."

"*Just* what I say," said Susan. "Well, come on then, let's start!"

"Er—," said Bill, "how *do* we start?"

"Exactly," said Charlotte, rather nastily the others considered. "After all, *you* can't get a search warrant and go barging into Miss Frame's shop like the police can."

"Well, actually," said Midge, "don't you think that the next move will come from the Mad Collector? If the Folding Letter didn't get behind the map by accident——"

"How could it get behind the map by accident?" Susan interrupted scornfully.

"Well, you never know," said Midge amiably. "But if it didn't, then the Mad Collector will come and try to get it back."

"After shooting us all dead, I suppose," said Charlotte hopelessly.

But, after all, it was Miss Frame who came. The arrival of the little dainty pink and white Dresden shepherdess on her bicycle and wearing an old raincoat was almost enough to set the Carmichaels off in another fit of the giggles, but the rather worrying secret of which they were in possession sobered them. Fortunately Aunt Lucy and Cousin Barbara had gone to Maidstone, so the Carmichaels and Susan were able to receive Miss Frame without giving away the secret of Aunt Lucy's birthday present. Miss Frame was almost in tears at having to ask for the map's return. "But, Mr. Smith—that's my partner you know— was quite upset, because he had promised, indeed *sold*, this map to another customer, an American gentleman who is coming down for it to-morrow —that was why it was in the back-shop, you see— and as this American gentleman has bought a lot of our maps it would never do to disappoint him. Mr. Smith is very sorry to disappoint *you*, but he hoped you would understand and sent this map of Kent in place of the other one and hoped that it would please Miss Carmichael because I told him, you know, that it was for your aunt's birthday. And between you and me and the gatepost, this is a very good bargain for you because this is a Christopher Saxton and *much* more expensive, but Mr. Smith was so sorry to disappoint you after the muddle I made this morning and he knew you particularly wanted Kent——"

"Oh, thank you very much, Miss Frame," said Charlotte, when she could get a chance to speak, "but I think we ought to pay the difference. At least I think we ought to if we had enough money, only I don't suppose we have."

Fortunately, however, Miss Frame wouldn't hear of this, and Bill clattered up his wooden stair to fetch down the road map.

To the others' horror he said, "We changed over the frames, Miss Frame—oh, how funny, ' the frames, Miss Frame,' I never thought of that before—but I'm sure the American gentleman won't mind."

"I'm sure he won't," said Miss Frame. She placed the map carefully in her bicycle basket, still thanking them. They went with her to the gate and she rode off.

"Bill," cried Charlotte as they watched her back disappearing along the road to Folding and Farthing Green, "in the name of goodness *why* did you tell her we'd changed the frames!"

"It was a subtle trap," said Bill, "to discover Miss Frame's innocence. If she had been in the secret of the stolen letter, she'd have gone into a flat spin when I said we'd changed the frames. But you see she didn't. She obviously didn't care."

"What a good idea!" said Susan admiringly. "I should never have thought of that! Oh, thank goodness she's innocent! That wicked Mad Collector is only using her darling wee shop for his own nefarious purposes!" Susan was delighted about this, and delighted too with the grand word that she had managed to introduce.

"But now," said Charlotte, alarmed, "what's the next step?" That Mad Collector will go madder when he gets the map back and there's no letter behind it! And he'll come charging down here and kill us!"

"That's what I'm hoping," said Bill complacently. "At least," he went on when Charlotte opened her mouth to protest, "not that he'll kill us, but that he'll come down here to get the other map and that we'll catch him in the act! He'll think that we somehow managed to change the maps without noticing the Letter—as we should have done if Susan hadn't gone poking her nose in—he won't imagine that we suspect him."

"Why not?" said Charlotte.

"Well, of course, by the way we've behaved," said Bill impatiently. "Miss Frame will go back and tell him that we were very nice about letting her have back the road map—no trouble at all. Then he'll discover that the Letter has gone and he'll somehow try to get it back."

"He won't just come and ask for the other map, will he?" said Susan anxiously.

"I don't see how he can try that dodge twice," said Bill. "Even to the little innocents that he thinks we are it would seem rather peculiar. If he does we'll tell Constable Bristow at once, of course, and stop him passing the map on to his

American customer. But I think that he'll try to steal it. I'll leave it out on the dressing-table after Aunt Lucy has said good night, just to make it easy for him."

"And I suppose," said Midge, "that we'll be wrapping up the parcel and handing it to him?"

"Oh, *no!*" cried Susan, who was sometimes rather literal, "I want to catch him!"

"You're welcome," said Charlotte. "You'll suffer no competition from me."

"Well, Charlotte," said Bill, "I'm sorry, but I'm afraid you'll have to help. My idea is that we should lie in wait for him in the dining-room, taking it in turns—two by two—to sleep."

Midge sighed. She loved her bed, and to be denied it for even one night was hard to bear.

Susan said excitedly, "But Bill, will he know to come in by the side door so that we can catch him?"

"Well, he won't exactly *know*, Susie you ass," said Bill patiently, "but if he has any sense he'll try the doors first, and he'll find the side door open."

"Oh, will he?" said Susan.

They spent a delightful evening laying their plans, and preparing lengths of clothes-line to tie up the Mad Collector, and a gag. Susan had once been bound and gagged herself, and she insisted on a gag for the first enemy of society whom she happened to encounter.

"Now, what about the sleeping rota?" said Bill, determined to do the thing in a business-like way.

"I suppose it has occurred to you," said

Charlotte, "that if once Midge gets to sleep nothing on this earth will wake her? Short of dynamite."

"And we haven't any dynamite," said Susan. "Bother."

"Well," said Midge, "if you think I'm going to stay awake all night just because I'm difficult to waken, you've got quite the wrong idea about how much I'll put up with."

"Midge and I can take the first two hours," said Susan. "From twelve—or whenever the old folk go to bed—until two."

"And it'll be *our* job to waken Midge," said Charlotte gloomily, "at four o'clock."

"Oh well," said Bill, determined to keep cheerful at all costs, "I dare say he'll come in the early part of the night."

"I dare say he won't come at all," said Midge. "What a sell *that* will be!"

CHAPTER TEN

SUSAN MAKES A MISTAKE

BUT THE Mad Collector came.

The watchers had almost given up hope. Susan and Midge had been wakened for their second duty and Midge was in a really horrible temper. Charlotte and Bill curled up on the cushions on the floor and covered themselves with the rugs which they had provided.

"Do shut up, Midge," whispered Bill. "We're all cold and stiff and fed-up. I must say," he added, "I never should have imagined from the books I've read that this sort of thing would be so dull."

"Isn't it *awful*," yawned Susan. "And the time goes so slowly. Oh, do shut *up*, Midge. Of course you can't put a light on and read."

"Well, it's impossible that I should keep awake," grumbled Midge. "Couldn't I go into the kitchen and make some tea or something?"

"If you *want* Cousin Barbara and Aunt Lucy to come down and see what's going on," whispered Charlotte, "I suppose you could."

But Susan said, "Actually, I don't see why she shouldn't, if she keeps quiet and doesn't light a candle. Only I'd rather have cocoa."

Bill and Charlotte gave in rather reluctantly, as it offended their idea of the fitness of things for a

member of the watch to go off in the middle to
make tea—or cocoa for that matter; only they
were obliged to confess that some hot cocoa
would cheer them up considerably and was worth
delaying their sleep.

"But be careful, Midge," begged Bill. "*Don't*
make a noise and spoil everything. And keep
Wendy quiet."

"Glory," said Midge, "I forgot Wendy! Won't
she bark like mad if he comes?"

"That big sweet lump of good-nature? She's
never been known to bark yet," said Charlotte.
"But be quick, Midge."

"And don't go to sleep in the kitchen," said
Susan.

Midge said nothing, but silently disappeared.
The others, crouched on the floor, said nothing
either. It was just after four. The old house
creaked and rustled in the stillness; before very
long the birds' dawn chorus would be beginning
and all hope of the Mad Collector's coming would
be over. And at that moment they heard a faint
sound. They all agreed afterwards that it was the
faint thump of Wendy flinging herself against
the kitchen door in welcome; a second or so later
they heard the unmistakable click of the back door
being carefully closed.

The Mad Collector must have pumped Miss
Frame to some purpose about the lie of the land;
he slipped across the little hall, a darker shadow
against the darkness, visible for one instant,
before a faint gleam of a shadowed torch and a
slight creak betrayed his presence on the back

stairs. The watchers knew what to do; they counted twenty slowly, then silently crept after him. They were so excited that they didn't hear the old stairs protesting as they crept up; ready to spring, they pushed open Bill's bedroom door.

They were met by the strong beam of a torch and a low sinister voice which said, "Come in quietly and shut the door. I've got a gun."

Susan's heart leapt with fear. Then it settled down again because she had been caught that way once before. "Pooh," she said, "it's easy to say 'I've got a gun'! On him, Bill——"

"Oh no," said the low sinister voice. "Look——!" The beam of the torch was directed away from them and on to a man's hand—and gleamed on a wicked-looking revolver. Bill, Charlotte and Susan came in quietly and shut the door.

"So it was a trap, was it?" said the Mad Collector nastily. "However, I don't feel inclined to fall into any footling trap to-night. I'm going to take the map and go—go where *you'll* never find me. You, boy—tie their legs and arms. And do it properly."

"What with?" said Bill sulkily.

"What were you going to tie me with?" said the Mad Collector. "Use that."

Bill reluctantly drew some clothes-rope out of his pocket and tied Charlotte and Susan hand and foot. Susan protested at one point that the rope was too tight; the Mad Collector came over and gave it a savage jerk. Susan was silent after that.

"Now tie your own legs," ordered the Collector.

He was bending over poor Bill, his last victim, tying his hands behind his back, when Midge crept in and hit him over the head with a frying-pan.

With a tiny grunt, the Mad Collector rolled over and lay across Bill's legs.

There was a whisper of joy and jubilation, but Midge said in a small squeak of horror, "Have I killed him?"

"I hope so," said Bill. "Midge, untie me, quickly!" But what with fright and the darkness Midge made no headway with Bill's hands at all. "Put the torch so that you can see what you're doing," said Bill impatiently. "He'll come to before we've got him tied up."

"How can he come too when he's dead?" said Midge.

"'Course he's not dead," said Bill. "Hurry up."

"I don't know how you can be sure," said Susan, "it was a most terrific wallop."

"Well, let's tie him up first and make sure afterwards," said Bill; and eventually they were all free and it was the turn of the Mad Collector to be bound hand and foot and gagged into the bargain. Charlotte gingerly picked up the revolver and put it under the mattress of Bill's bed. She was quite terrified that Bill would grab it and shoot them all dead by mistake. She put the Folding Letter there too.

"What now?" said Susan, thinking hopefully of the cocoa that Midge had been making.

"Well *now*," said Bill, going through the pockets of the still inert Mr. Smith, "we must go over to the shop at Farthing Green and collect the rest of the manuscripts—oh good, here are his keys."

"I suppose the manuscripts will be there?" said Charlotte.

"I should think so," said Bill, "he does all his map framing there."

"What do we do with the body, which isn't a body, thank goodness?" said Midge, giving Mr. Smith a poke with her foot.

Nobody had thought of that.

"We must just leave him here," said Bill.

"And give Cousin Barbara heart failure when she comes in to waken you in the morning," said Charlotte. "Though it's a miracle that she hasn't heard something of this hullabaloo already——"

"I don't think it is, really," said Midge, "the walls are so thick and this room is right away from all the others."

"Don't you think we should telephone Mr. Bristow and get him to come over?" said Charlotte. "I'll be happier when the Mad Collector is locked up."

"But we want to go and find the manuscripts on our own," objected Bill, "and Mr. Bristow would never let us. Let's write a note for Cousin Barbara and ask *her* to telephone Mr. Bristow. That'll give us a start."

So Bill hunted out a piece of paper and a pencil, and Charlotte wrote: ' Don't get a fright, but the Mad Collector is lying bound and gagged in Bill's room. Please telephone Mr. Bristow and ask him to remove him. We'll be back soon.' Then she gently slipped the note under Cousin Barbara's door.

As no one seemed to listen to Susan's murmurs about cocoa she, with admirable foresight as it turned out, filled her pockets and a paper-bag with biscuits and rock-cakes and apples. She would have taken a jug of milk too, but didn't see how she could manage it on her bicycle.

It was beginning to get light. They took their bicycles out of the shed and rode off in the direction of Farthing Green in the wildest spirits. All thoughts of tiredness had entirely left them, and even Midge burst into song when they were well out of earshot of the farm.

When they reached Miss Frame's at Farthing Green they put their bicycles out of sight behind the little antique shop.

"Now do be quiet," said Bill. "We don't want the Dresden shepherdess nosing over here before we've found what we want."

"And for goodness' sake," said Midge, "remember the mat!"

"Oh help," said Susan, "what a good thing you mentioned it, for I'd have stood on it, sure as a gun!"

"Don't talk about guns," shuddered Charlotte. "It'll be a long time before I can even think about guns without feeling sick."

Having looked around for curious onlookers, of which there were none, fortunately, at that time in the morning, Bill unlocked the door, and they all slipped inside. "Quick, into the back shop," said Bill, we don't want to be seen——"

They edged cautiously past the china-laden shelves, round the little show-case which held patch-boxes and old silver, into the minute room of which the back premises consisted. Here they found frames, boards, glue, sheets of glass—all the paraphernalia for framing the old maps; they found the old maps themselves, but of the ancient manuscripts they found not a trace. They searched every corner—it didn't take long, because the room was about six feet square. Susan was, with difficulty restrained from tearing up the floor-boards.

"Don't be dotty, Susan," said Charlotte. "You can see that floor hasn't been disturbed for years."

Susan sat back on her heels and stared up at Charlotte. "Listen," she said, "I've just thought of something——"

"What are we supposed to do, wave flags?" said Midge nastily, this final disappointment having soured her temper.

Susan ignored this. "No, but *listen*," she said. "D'you remember when we came for the map the first time and the shop was shut and I looked through the window and saw Mr. Smith?" The others said that they remembered, and what about it? "Well," said Susan, "that little show-case was moved to one side and the carpet was rolled back!"

"Was it!" said Bill, again all eagerness. "Well, let's move the little show-case and roll the carpet back——"

They pushed back into the shop. Bill and Charlotte carefully moved the little show-case.

Susan put her paper bag of rock-cakes and biscuits which she had been clutching all this time, on the floor and Midge and she rolled back the small square of carpet. In the floor was a trap-door, secured by a new-looking lock. "Oh, Bill," said Susan, "don't say that you haven't got the key!"

Bill hastily fumbled through the bunch of keys which he had taken from Mr. Smith's pocket; there was a great sigh of relief from the onlooking girls when he fitted a key in the lock and turned it. Bill and Charlotte lifted back the trap-door; a steep flight of steps led to the cellar below. They crowded down the steep steps; Bill found a light switch and snapped it on. In an old chest of drawers, unobtrusively mingled with old maps, old water-colours and worthless prints, they found ancient parchments, manuscripts with crabbed old English script, vellum lovingly illuminated by medieval monks. Naturally, the children could not identify them, but that they were the proceeds of previous robberies by the Mad Collector they were certain. "Goodness," said Susan wildly, "I expect they're all old manuscripts that are absolutely priceless! I expect they're all written by Shakespeare!"

"Well, hardly," said Charlotte, "but who cares? We've found them!"

"Oh help," thought Susan, "I think I'll *die* with excitement! And actually, I *know* I'll die with hunger. What did I do with that poke of biscuits?" She climbed up the ladder-like stairs and retrieved the paper bag from the floor of the shop. It was by now full daylight Susan saw as she glanced up at the windows. "If anyone happened to look in," she thought suddenly, "and saw that trap-door raised, they'd wonder what was going on. I'd better shut it." She went down a step or two, with her paper bag, and cautiously shut the trap-door above her head. The others had, with great care, sorted out the manuscripts and put them between cardboard as a protection.

"Well, let's go," said Charlotte. "We'll take these straight to Constable Bristow."

"How soon will we get the reward?" said Susan. "Not to-day, I suppose."

"Ass," said Midge, "of course not. The insurance company will have to make sure these are the genuine article before they pay us."

"Five thousand pounds!" murmured Susan, in a happy dream.

"Divided by four, remember," said Midge.

Bill had gone up the ladder and was pushing sharply against the trap-door. "Susie," he said, "did you shut this trap-door?"

"Yes," said Susan, "I didn't fancy people looking in the windows and seeing it open——"

"Well, give us the keys," said Bill. "Where are they?"

Susan came out of her happy dream. "They're on the floor of the shop," she whispered.

CHAPTER ELEVEN

MISS FRAME TO THE RESCUE

THEY SAT on the floor, on the ladder, and abused Susan.

"Well, I'm terribly sorry," said Susan abjectly, when they had run out of rude adjectives, "I just completely forgot about the keys."

"I suppose you thought your middle name was Aladdin," said Bill, "and all you had to do was say, 'Open Sesame!'"

"Even Aladdin forgot the magic word," said Susan. "Not that that's any excuse," she added hastily, as Bill turned rather menacingly on her. "I don't suppose anyone would like a biscuit?" she said, sniffing dolefully.

Her cousins relented sufficiently to help themselves out of Susan's by now sordid-looking paper bag.

"We'll *need* some sustenance before we're rescued," said Charlotte gloomily. "How long d'you think it will be before Miss Frame opens her shop?"

"Some days she doesn't open it at all," said Susan.

"If you take my advice," Midge whispered, "you'll keep quiet for a little."

Susan subsided, and the others discussed what time it was likely to be—no one having a watch—

and what time it was likely to be when Miss Frame saw fit to open her shop.

"It can't be more than about seven now, I should think," said Midge, "and is it likely that Miss Frame will have any customers before ten?"

"Perhaps she'll come in earlier to dust," said Charlotte.

"Three hours at least," said Midge. "Well, I'm going to lie down on the floor and sleep. After all, I didn't have any scarcely last night. Lie down, Susie, and let me put my head on your tummy."

They decided that it was the least Susan could do, after the jam she had got them in, to lie down and let them *all* put their heads on her tummy. Susan meekly did so. "Ugh, well," she thought, "I'll probably suffocate or something with all that weight on me—and then they'll be sorry——"

Perhaps they all slept; Midge certainly did; anyway, it didn't seem terribly long until they heard light footsteps above them.

"Oh, *there* she is, thank goodness!" whispered Charlotte. "Now we must be cautious or we'll frighten the poor little thing out of her wits."

A voice called sharply from above. "Who's down there? Is that you, Wilfred?"

"Oh, Miss Frame!" called Charlotte, running up the steps, "don't be alarmed, but it's us, the Carmichaels—we're locked in!"

"Good gracious me!" twittered the voice of Miss Frame, "however did you get down there? Wait a minute and I'll let you out——"

In a minute, as she promised, the trap-door was

lifted, and the little pink and white face of Miss Frame peered anxiously down at them. "Whatever are you doing down there?" she said. "Wait, I'll come down——" She came carefully down the ladder. "Now," she said, "tell me——!"

"Miss Frame," said Charlotte, gently taking her hand, "we've got some very bad news for you I'm afraid."

Bill said, "Miss Frame, are you very fond of Mr. Smith?"

"Well," said Miss Frane, looking bewildered, "he's my cousin——"

"I think you had better sit down," said Midge gently.

Miss Frame allowed herself to be seated on one of the steps of the ladder. Susan felt that she could hardly bear this touching scene.

"Go on, Charlotte," said Midge.

"Miss Frame," said Charlotte, not quite knowing how to begin, "you know all these robberies of valuable manuscripts that there have been in Kent, and the papers called the thief the Mad Collector on account of his stealing such mad things?"

Miss Frame looked wildly at Charlotte and nodded.

"Well, Miss Frame," said Charlotte, "I'm terribly, terribly sorry, but the Mad Collector is Mr. Smith!"

Miss Frame jumped to her feet with a curious expression on her pretty face. "How *can* you say such a thing?" she demanded.

"It's true, I'm afraid," said Charlotte compassionately. "He's in the hands of the police by now—at least I hope he is—and the manuscripts are here—nine of them!"

"Where?" said Miss Frame. "Let me see——"

Bill lifted the bundle of cardboard from the corner where he had carefully put it, and laid it on the little chest of drawers for Miss Frame to look at the manuscripts.

She bent over them, hiding her face. "It's dreadful," she whispered, "I can't believe it." She rubbed the back of her hand across her eyes.

"Oh," cried Midge, unable to bear it any longer, "please, *please* don't be unhappy about it! It's not your fault, Miss Frame! *You* had nothing to do with it——"

"I should have seen—I should have stopped it somehow," said Miss Frame brokenly.

"How could you?" said Midge. "And look, Miss Frame," she went on eagerly, "the reward—we'll share it with you to pay off the mortgage on your little shop! And if that isn't enough, then you must have it all!"

"Ah! Such kindness!" said Miss Frame in a sad little voice. "But it won't pay off the shame, the disgrace——" She turned over the old manuscripts with her soft little white hands. "Where's the Folding Letter?" she murmured.

"Oh," said Bill, "that's safe under my mattress at Apple-tree Farm. That's how we caught him——"

Susan, who was standing behind Miss Frame, surreptitiously wiping her eyes, suddenly stopped stock-still with her handkerchief to her face. The others were relating, as gently as possible, the story of Mr. Smith's capture to Miss Frame. Susan, unnoticed, crept quietly up the ladder—and then came down again.

"—So you see," Charlotte finished, you *mustn't* blame yourself, Miss Frame, it had absolutely nothing to do with you, but there's no doubt about it that he is the Mad Collector—I mean, there are the manuscripts, as final proof, if any more proof were needed——"

"Oh, the manuscripts, yes!" exclaimed Miss Frame, "the beautiful manuscripts! Oh, children, I shan't have a minute's peace until they're under lock and key! I have a little safe over in the cottage, we'll put them there——" She picked up the manuscripts carefully. "Come along now," she said. "Just let me get up this horrid ladder, I'm rather wobbly on ladders."

"Let me take the manuscripts for you, Miss Frame," offered Bill.

"Oh, thank you, my dear, but I'm almost up now," said Miss Frame. She was safely up and Charlotte began to climb the ladder. There was a sudden crash as the trap-door slammed into place.

"Now you brats can stay there and *rot*," said the voice of the Dresden shepherdess.

CHAPTER TWELVE

SUSAN REDEEMS HERSELF

THERE WAS a stunned silence in the cellar. Then Charlotte ran up the steps and banged on the trap-door. "Miss Frame, Miss Frame!" she called. "The trap-door has slammed! Let us out!"

Midge said savagely, "She's double-crossed us! She's in it with Mr. Smith!"

Charlotte turned from her useless hammering and sat helplessly on one of the steps. "But, but how could she? She was crying!"

"Crying my foot!" said Bill. "She put on an act! And now she's got away with the manuscripts!"

Midge turned furiously on Susan. "And what d'you think you're standing there grinning at?" she demanded. "What is there to grin at, I'd like to know?"

"This," said Susan. She put her hand in her pocket and began tossing up and catching Mr. Smith's bunch of keys.

"But it's the keys!" said Charlotte stupidly, "that you left on the floor! How did *you* get them?"

"I crept up and got them when you were all looking at the manuscripts and crying," Susan said. "I guessed "—she said. She couldn't help feeling a little bit pleased, but she tried not to

show it, for after all it only made up for her
stupidity which had landed them in the mess in
the first place. "I guessed when she asked where
the Folding Letter was—how did she know about
the Folding Letter unless she knew everything?"

"Well, come *on*!" shrieked Bill. "What are we
waiting for? She'll get away——"

"Wait, wait!" said Midge. "We can't go
charging out like bulls in a china-shop "—no one
even stopped to giggle at the simile—"we must
have a plan of campaign!"

"One of us must run up to the Mill-House and
telephone Mr. Bristow," said Charlotte, who had
apparently got her breath back, and who was
doubly incensed at Miss Frame on account of
having been completely taken in by her pathetic
behaviour. "Maybe Mrs. Forester has a gardener
or somebody who will come down and help us
capture her——"

"We don't need any help," said Bill savagely.

No one seemed anxious for the comparatively
dull job of telephoning the police, but Susan said
at last, "Ugh, come on, we're wasting time—I'll
go—you three creep in and take her by surprise."

They unlocked the trap-door and bundled out
pell-mell into the little shop. "Don't forget the
mat!" shrieked Charlotte.

"Oh, thank you," gasped Susan, leaning over
and unlocking the door and leaping over the mat,
"I would *never* have remembered and the bell
would have given us away completely——!"

As the others prepared to make a sort of Red
Indian assault on the cottage, Susan ran round the

back of the shop and grabbed her bicycle. "It'll be quicker than walking up to the Mill-House," she thought, and that thought saved the day, for as she came to the edge of the road and glanced up and down for traffic she saw a small figure carrying a brief-case and hurrying up the hill to the bus stop, and in the other direction, the bus approaching.

"Oh help, oh *help*!" thought Susan. "She'll catch the bus! I'll never reach her before it comes! Oh help, oh help! Midge! Charlotte! Bill!" she yelled. "She's at the bus stop!" and flinging her bicycle wildly into the middle of the road, she turned and ran up the hill after Miss Frame.

The bus driver, having no room in that narrow road to swerve round the bicycle, drew up with a jerk and a grind of brakes. The passengers twittered excitedly at each other and began to alight. The driver climbed down off his cab grumbling savagely and shaking his fist at Susan. But Susan didn't care. Her hand was firmly on the handle of the brief-case, which Miss Frame was trying to drag out of her grasp, and the Carmichaels were pounding up the hill to her aid.

Well, the situation took a little sorting out, what with the accusations of Susan and the Carmichaels, and the rather hysterical denials of Miss Frame, and the shouting of the bus passengers, some being firmly on Miss Frame's side and the rest being equally firmly on the side of the children, added to which was the fury of the driver, although this became gradually mollified as the excitement rose. Just, however, when it looked as if nothing would settle the matter except a free fight between the rival factions, the miraculous appearance of Mr. Bristow and the sergeant from Folding settled it; and the passengers had the unwonted thrill of seeing Miss Frame, looking plaintive and ill-used, taken into custody, to the muttered and mostly irrelevant exclamations of "Serve her right!" "Poor little thing!" "You can tell by looking at her that she wouldn't hurt a fly!" "Lock 'er up!" "It's them nasty children as I'd lock up!" "It's always the same—one law for the rich and another for the pore!" "Spare the rod and spoil the child, *I* say!"

The Carmichaels were beginning to suffer from reaction, and Susan's embarrassment at the publicity of the scene was becoming acute when Constable Bristow whispered to them, "I'd cut along home if I was you. Your auntie's in a fine taking with the burglar on the floor and you gone and your beds not slept in and all. Shall I ask Sarge to give you a lift back in the police-car?"

"Oh *no*!" murmured Charlotte, "I couldn't bear to be near Miss Frame. Besides, we have our bikes, but thanks all the same."

"How did you get here, Mr. Bristow?" asked Bill. "It seemed like a miracle."

"Oh," said Mr. Bristow in high good humour, "*I* guessed you'd be coming along to the shop when Mrs. Trent told me who the joker on the floor was. So I phoned for a car from Maidstone and picked up the Sarge, I thought he'd like to see what was doing, and we came along here after we'd locked our friend up——"

"Are the manuscripts all safe?" said Susan, suddenly anxious about the reward.

"Safe as the bank!" said Mr. Bristow, slapping the brief-case. Then he raised his voice and said firmly, "Come along then, move along there, now——" and the bus and the bus passengers and half the population of Farthing Green who had by this time gathered round, moved along. . . .

There were more scenes of wonderment and agitation when the Carmichaels and Susan got back to Apple-tree Farm. Then they suddenly remembered that it was Aunt Lucy's birthday and presented the maps, to her incredulous delight.

"And if it hadn't been for your maps, Aunt Lucy, we'd never have discovered the Mad Collector," said Susan, and then the whole story had to be recounted amid exclamations of amazement and horror to Cousin Barbara and Aunt Lucy and Belle and Mary and Robert, who had assembled to hear the excitement. When they came to the bit about the gun, Aunt Lucy behaved in a very agitated manner and forbade them ever to catch a burglar again in their lives, and they all assured her that as far as they knew they never would, because after all it wasn't a thing that happened every day; and Aunt Lucy wanted to know where the gun was now, and Bill said that it was under his mattress if no one had moved it, and Aunt Lucy gave a little cry of alarm and Cousin Barbara begged her to calm herself, and said that she would go and retrieve the gun and put it in a safe place because she knew about guns. Bill wanted to know what they should do with the Folding Letter which was also under the mattress when that point was solved by the arrival of Sir Hubert, advised of the recent events by Constable Bristow, and come in person to thank the children. They recounted the events of the night once more and handed over the Folding Letter, which Sir Hubert, in a burst of gratitude, seemed on the point of presenting to them until brought to his senses by Aunt Lucy, who reminded him of the store Miss Folding set by the Letter.

"Quite right, quite right," said Sir Hubert. "Never can see anything in it myself. Not pretty. Interesting of course, but not nice to look at. Not like my Constable. Insurance fellahs will see you about the reward, but Miss Folding will want to give you some little present. Come to tea to-morrow and meet her. Shouldn't wonder if she'll have some little china trifle for you, young lady," he said to Charlotte. "Need to see what you others like," and he stumped off in high good humour with his spaniel.

Charlotte blushed with pleasure.

"Will having a present from Miss Folding affect the reward?" said Susan in what seemed to her cousins a very grasping way and quite unlike her.

"Of course not," said Bill. "It was the insurance company who offered the reward——"

"What *is* all this about the reward?" said Midge. "You keep on about it, Susie——"

"Well," said Susan apologetically, "Charlotte and her collection of china that she hasn't got— I did want to buy her that wee poodle; and I'd like the Coalport jug for Mummy to go with her tea-set, and this reward is the only way I can see of ever having fourteen pounds to buy them with!"

"Oh," said Charlotte; and Midge said that the little antique-shop would probably have to be sold up to pay for the expenses of Miss Frame's defence when she came to trial, if she had any defence, and maybe Susan would get the things a bit cheaper.

After these excitements, it was quite useless for Aunt Lucy to suggest that they should all go to bed and try to make up the sleep that they had lost the night before. Charlotte and Susan said they weren't sleepy so that it would be perfectly silly to go to bed, and Midge said that although she *had* been so sleepy that she nearly fell off her bike coming back from Farthing Green, she must have got her second wind or something because now she felt as fresh as a daisy; and Bill didn't say anything but quietly disappeared in case Aunt Lucy should get too insistent about this bed idea. But Aunt Lucy only said oh well, in a helpless sort of way, and Cousin Barbara said that it wasn't worth going to bed now anyway, because they were having lunch early, and the children could have a rest after lunch before Evelyn came; and she bustled off to ice Aunt Lucy's birthday cake, which had been overlooked in the general excitement, and Aunt Lucy went to lay the table for lunch and took Charlotte with her.

Susan gazed at Midge, wide-eyed with consternation. "Midge!" she said. "With all this bother about the Mad Collector going on, I completely forgot about Belle! And I wanted to present Mrs. Forester with her long-lost nieces—and nephew—this afternoon!"

"Oh well," said Midge, "you'll have to postpone it for a day or two. After all, Mrs. Forester doesn't know the treat you had in store for her."

Susan said, nor listening to Midge, "There must be *some* simple way of proving it. Midge, will you keep guard in case Belle or Mary or Robert comes in while I do a bit of telephoning?"

"Who are you going to telephone?" said Midge anxiously.

"Well, Mrs. Forester, of course," said Susan, "but don't worry, I'll be the soul of tact and not give the show away at all."

"There's no show to give away," said Midge. "She'll only think you're dotty if you ring her up."

"No, she won't," said Susan. "I've worked it all out. Do watch out for Belle and the others!"

Mary and Robert had gone with Bill to watch the farm boys who were cutting the hedge round the apple orchard, and finding a bird's nest at every yard, practically. Bill and the other two were beside themselves at these pleasures, and the boys' hedging was much hampered by constant stops to lift Mary and Robert to see into the nests where the eggs, the blue of the hedge-sparrow and the brown-spotted chaffinch's, lay cosily. Bill, of course, was quite big enough to see for himself either by standing on tiptoe or by climbing the ladder that the boys were using; the only trouble being that once he overbalanced in his eagerness and fell into the hedge and scratched himself half to death without, fortunately, doing any damage to the nest.

Back in the house, Midge reluctantly kept guard, although it wasn't really necessary as Belle was busy in the kitchen polishing silver for the afternoon's tea-party, and Susan rang up Mrs. Forester. Contrary to Midge's expectations Susan was quite tactful.

"Oh, Mrs. Forester," she said, "I thought you'd like to hear about this morning's affair at first hand although of course we'll tell you the whole story when you come over this afternoon." She then gave Mrs. Forester the gist of the events, of which Mrs. Forester had already heard a garbled and alarming version, and Mrs. Forester thanked her for calling and said that she never would have thought it of Miss Frame.

"Oh, and by the way, Mrs. Forester," said Susan innocently, "where did your nieces live in Africa because my mother and father are there just now and I thought I could just mention it when I write and they might be able to find out something——"

"Why, Susan, how sweet of you to take such an interest," Mrs. Forester's voice sounded rather amused. "Africa is a big place, you know! But they lived in Kenya, near a place called Nakuru."

"I suppose that Africa *is* a big place," Susan

agreed sadly. "Had your nieces any distinguishing marks at all?" she went on.

"Oh, my dear, *no*, not a birthmark or two left feet among them," said Mrs. Forester. "Sickening, isn't it? But I guess I'd know them if I saw them."

Susan then guilefully mentioned the morning's excitement again, and allowed Mrs. Forester to ring off.

Midge took a book and went out to the summer-house. The rockery was a blaze of purple and blue and violet and pink, and polyanthus filled the flower-bed beyond the pergola. She took a deck-chair and lay in the sun out of the wind. The garden was so peaceful after the disturbances of the night; just by lifting her eyes from her book she could see all the glorious masses of colour, and the ring of forget-me-nots round the rose-bed . . . and the green lawn, daisy-starred, and the japonica against the wall and the lilac trees in bud . . . She could see the beautiful old gable of the house and its slightly crooked windows . . . Swallows darted across the lawn, and the sparrows chattered busily round their nests in the eaves . . . "I wish," thought Midge drowsily, "I wish I could live here always and just do nothing but look at all these heavenly things for ever "—and Midge shut her eyes and went to sleep.

Susan meanwhile peeped in at Belle in the kitchen and saw that she was still occupied with the silver. She felt guiltily that she ought to help her, but she stifled this feeling and went out by the side door where the patch of wallflowers smelt divinely in the sun. She was feeling slightly light-headed with lack of sleep. She walked along the side of the cobbled yard and round the oast-houses, between the kitchen garden and the trim rows of currant bushes to the apple orchard. The blossom was really out now, and she stopped every little while to gaze at the pink and white against the blue sky. She found Mary reading a book and leaning against the trunk of a tree, obviously because Belle had dared her to lie on the damp grass.

"What's the book?" said Susan.

Mary looked up rather blankly. "*The Green Fairy Book*," she said, coming reluctantly out of her fairy world. "Mrs. Trent lent it to me."

"Oh, I had those when I was a kid," said Susan. "*The Green* and *The Blue Fairy Book* and *The Crimson*. . . . Where's everybody," she said.

"Somewhere about," said Mary vaguely.

"Mary," said Susan, who really didn't see any reason for further beating about the bush, "where did you live in Africa?"

Mary stiffened. She kicked at a tuft of grass. "I can't remember," she muttered.

Susan sighed. "I wish you could," she said. "I'd like to help you——"

"I can't tell you," Mary said desperately. "Belle said that if I told you anything we'd have to go back to——" she stopped, her eyes wide and frightened.

"Oh dear," thought Susan, "what *is* Belle's secret? I should have been finding it out instead of gadding about catching Collectors——" It didn't occur to her for one minute that Belle might prefer to be left in possession of her secret, whatever it might be; Belle needed help, and how was Susan to help her if she didn't know what the matter was? "Mary," she said, in one last despairing effort, "you haven't lost any relations, have you? An aunt, for instance?"

If it was results Susan wanted, she got them. Mary went quite white, and a look of terror came into her eyes. She shut her book. "I must go and find Belle," she muttered, and hurried off across the orchard.

Susan felt quite ill with guilt as she saw Mary's hunted look. "I just don't understand it," she said to herself. "Why should she be frightened of an aunt she's never seen? But all the same, it's ridiculous that they should *be* so frightened. If I could only find out what the trouble is, then Cousin Barbara could put it right, or Aunt Lucy——"

She wandered around under the apple trees until she came on the hedging party, and climbing the little steps duly examined the latest discovery in nests. The farm boys were quite resolute about not allowing even one egg to be taken, Susan noted, although she couldn't help wondering if the poor frightened birds would ever come back to homes so disturbed.

Robert was saying, "I should like very much to have some birds' eggs, but of course I know that we mustn't take them. But if I found one on the ground I could have it, couldn't I?"

"Did you go bird's-nesting in Africa?" said Susan.

"'Course not," said Robert, shocked. "It's wicked to rob birds' nests."

"I didn't mean *rob* them," said Susan. "Where did you live in Africa, Robert?"

Robert gave her a glance from his dark eyes. "In the jungle!" he whispered in a mysterious voice. "And the lions used to come right up to the *stoep* and look in at the windows! And I killed a dangerous snake once!"

"I bet you didn't," said Bill.

"I bet you a million pounds I did," said Robert.

"Ugh, it's hopeless," thought Susan in disgust, and made her way back to the house.

CHAPTER THIRTEEN

THE LONG-LOST NIECES—AND NEPHEW

SHE WENT up the funny little ladder-steps to her attic bedroom to find the book that she was reading. She found Belle instead, putting a vase of fresh wallflowers on the muslin-frilled dressing-table.

"'Water, water wallflower, growing up so high,'" sang Susan.

"'We are all maidens and we must all die.
    Except Belle Smith, the youngest of us all,
    She can dance and she can sing and she can
        knock us all down——'
That's what we used to sing when we were kids —d'you know it, Belle?" she said. "It's a singing game."

"No," said Belle shortly. Her hand was on the latch of the door.

"Ugh, Belle," said Susan in despair, "I wish you'd let me help you. I wish you'd tell me what's worrying you——"

"I wish you'd mind your own business," said Belle, goaded at last to rudeness. "There's nothing worrying me except you——" and she jerked open the door in her anxiety to be off and clattered down the little ladder. But her haste was her undoing. Her heel caught on a step, she lost her balance, and with no rail to save her she crashed to the foot of the stairs and lay motionless.

Susan darted to her bedroom door. "Oh help!" she gasped when she saw the still, huddled figure. "Oh, *Belle*!" She leapt down the little stairs and knelt down by Belle. Belle's eyes were closed and she was deathly pale. "Oh help, oh help," thought Susan, "I've killed her! I did it, poking and prying——" And at that instant she saw the ring. Attached to its thin gold chain, pulled out in Belle's fall, it lay against Belle's jumper. Susan just couldn't resist; she gently picked up the pretty little ring and read inside: *D.R.S. to A.M.G.* and a date. She pushed the ring back inside Belle's jumper. She ran to the top of the front stairs and called, "Cousin Barbara! Aunt Lucy! Come *quickly*!" She went to the bathroom for water. Cousin Barbara, alarmed by the crash, came hurrying up the back stairs.

"What is it? What's the matter?" she called. "I heard a crash——"

"It's Belle," cried Susan, coming out of the bathroom with a glass of water and a wet sponge, "she fell down the attic stairs and I think she's dead——"

"Dead!" said Cousin Barbara. "Nonsense, she's sitting up!"

Belle was sitting up, holding her head with both hands.

"My poor child," said Cousin Barbara, "are you all right?"

"Oh, Belle, oh, Belle," said Susan, "I thought you were dead!"

Belle muttered, "I'm so sorry, Mrs. Trent, making such a fool of myself. I must have knocked myself out for a second. I'm quite all right——" She struggled to her feet, ignoring Susan's helping hand.

"Well, you may be all right," said Cousin Barbara, " but you just come and lie down on my bed for a little. I'll telephone the doctor——"

"The doctor!" gasped Belle. "The doctor mustn't come! I must get home before—I mean I must get home after I've washed up the lunch dishes! And it's time now to put the potatoes on—I'll go and do it!"

"Ah-ha!" thought the amateur detective by her side. "She must get home before Mrs. Forester comes, she was going to say! I'm right—there *is* some connection, I know it!"

Cousin Barbara was saying, "Oh bother the potatoes, you're going to lie down! Susan can put on the potatoes."

"Yes, of course, Cousin Barbara," said Susan reluctantly. She much preferred herself in the role of ministering angel, getting information out of her patient when in a state weakened by her fall, but she went off obediently to put on the potatoes. Cousin Barbara made Belle lie down, covered her with a rug, bathed the place on her forehead, where a lump was rising, with witch hazel. Belle looked sullen, but submitted.

"Dr. Freeman often passes here about half-past twelve on his way home for lunch," said Cousin

Barbara, "I'll get the children to try and catch him."

Dr. Freeman was duly caught, and having examined Belle he set everyone's mind at rest by pronouncing that there was no concussion, nothing to worry about, and that she could get up, seeing that she seemed so set on it.

When Mary and Robert were on holiday, Cousin Barbara had insisted that all three should wait at the farm for lunch each day, for which Belle had tried to make up by working harder than ever and by washing and drying the dishes before Cousin Barbara could even help her. This day, however, she seemed in such a hurry to be cleared up that she practically snatched the plates from them while they were still thinking of second helpings, and ignored Cousin Barbara's protests that she wasn't in a fit state to wash dishes. Cousin Barbara, however, did refuse to allow her to lay the table for tea or make sandwiches. "Why don't you wait here for tea, anyway, Belle?" she said. "It would save you getting tea for the children and you ought to have a 'quiet afternoon.'"

"Oh *no*, thank you," gasped Belle. "Oh no, I couldn't do that! Please may I go now, if there's nothing else I can do?"

Cousin Barbara sighed and said, "Oh, all right, off you go——"

Susan watched Belle off the premises, then made a dart for the telephone.

"Mrs. Forester will think I'm potty," she said to Midge, "but I can't help that. Watch out for

Cousin Barbara, or she'll think I'm potty too, ringing her up. But I can't wait to know——"

"I don't suppose you care that I think you're potty too?" said Midge. "Although I must say," she added in fairness, "I'm beginning to be convinced that there must be *some* connection between Belle and Mrs. Forester, with Belle in her usual flat spin to get away before Mrs. Forester arrives. But what I can't make out is why Belle should *be* so anxious to avoid her. *I* should at least want to have a look at my long-lost aunt. For curiosity, if nothing else."

"'Sh!" said Susan peremptorily. "Oh, Mrs. Forester, it's Susan Lyle again—oh, yes, thanks—none the worse. Mrs. Forester, I'm sorry to bother you, but could you tell me what your sister's engagement ring looked like?" This was obviously such an unexpected question to Mrs. Forester that Susan had to repeat it three times before she took it in. "A sapphire surrounded by little diamonds? Is a sapphire that blue stone? Yes, that's right, and Mrs. Forester, did it have anything written inside?"

Mrs. Forester, who was a kindly and patient woman, said, "Yes, it had initials as far as I can remember. *D.S. to A.M.G.*, I suppose, and the date——"

"Could it be *D.R.S.*?" said Susan, scarcely daring to breathe.

"I guess so," said Mrs. Forester. "His middle name was Robert——"

"Oh—oh—oh," Susan gave a long sigh of joy. "Well, Mrs. Forester, don't get excited, but I think we've found your long-lost nieces—and nephew!"

"What did she say?" said Midge, when Susan had put down the receiver.

"Well, nothing, for a second," said Susan, "and then she said that I'd better tell her all about it when she came over, and if it wasn't a nuisance she'd come right away. So I hope Cousin Barbara is ready for her."

"We'd better warn Cousin Barbara and Aunt Lucy," Midge said. "And won't we look a couple of clots if it's all a mistake?"

"It isn't a mistake," said Susan positively. "But must we tell Cousin Barbara and the others just yet?"

"I think we must give them a hint at least," said Midge. "Or else it's going to be a considerable shock to them when Mrs. Forester comes charging in demanding her nieces."

"Yes, but have we time?" said Susan. "I bet you they'll take some convincing."

"Leave it to me," said Midge. So she went to Cousin Barbara and Aunt Lucy who were cutting sandwiches and gossiping in the kitchen. "Cousin Barbara," she said, "we think that Belle knows something about Mrs. Forester's long-lost nieces——"

Cousin Barbara looked up with her bread-knife in mid-air. "How on earth could my little Belle know about Mrs. Forester's long-lost nieces, as you call them?" she said.

"It's a long story," began Midge.

"This wouldn't be Susan's helping hand at work again, would it?" said Aunt Lucy suspiciously.

"Well, yes," Midge admitted, "but honestly, Aunt Lucy, I think there's something in it. So Susie and I are going over to Belle's cottage to sort of prepare her for Mrs. Forester's visit, and could you bring Mrs. Forester there when she comes? It's a nice walk, even if there's nothing in it," she added in a sudden access of panic. "And by the way, Mrs. Forester is coming over from Farthing Green right away."

The two grown-ups shrieked. "Right *away*!" said Cousin Barbara. "We're not nearly ready!"

"Has Charlotte done the table?" said Aunt Lucy, getting flustered.

"I'll go and see," said Midge. Charlotte had done the table and was reclining in the summer-house, listening open-mouthed to Susan's resumé of events to date.

"I just can't believe it," she said when Midge came on the scene. "You know what you are, Susie, you've made it up!"

"I have not, then," said Susan. "Have I, Midge?"

Midge admitted cautiously that there seemed to be some grounds for thinking that Belle was indeed Mrs. Forester's lost niece. "Only," she added, "there are a few things that want explaining. I mean, Belle doesn't appear to have lost an aunt—and why is Belle terrified of anyone finding out about her past history, because she is, you know——"

"She certainly is," Susan agreed feelingly. "*And* Mary—*and* Robert."

"And," went on Midge, "why is she terrified of meeting Mrs. Forester? Anyway, Susie and I thought that we'd better go and warn her that she's about to meet Mrs. Forester. Are you coming?"

"Me?" squeaked Charlotte. "I hate to think what'll happen to you when you go and tell that little wild-cat that you've arranged a meeting with Mrs. Forester! I'll come along later and render first-aid."

As usual, Belle didn't seem very pleased to see them. She grudgingly asked them in; Mary and Robert came in from the garden.

"You tell her, Susie," said Midge.

Susan, now that it had come to the point, was frankly terrified of Belle's black brows and sullen expression. "No, go on—*you* tell her," she muttered.

"Tell me *what*?" snapped Belle. "What *is* this?"

Susan took a deep breath. "Belle," she said, "don't get a shock, but we think we have found your Aunt Evelyn——" She trailed off into silence at the sight of Belle's stricken face.

"You've *what*?" said Belle.

"We, we think we've found your Aunt Evelyn," said Susan in a small voice. "She's coming to see you in a little——"

Belle's face was white, the bruise from that morning's fall standing out ugly and discoloured. "How dare you, how *dare* you come poking your nose in and doing this to us?" she said.

"Belle," said Susan, who was feeling horribly sick, "I didn't mean—I didn't mean to upset you. Mrs. Forester had lost her nieces—I was trying to help——"

"To help!" said Belle contemptuously. "You've been poking and prying ever since you came here, trying to find out about us—you were even mean enough to try and pump the children. Well, now I'll tell you! We lived with my aunt for two months after we came to England, and I hated my aunt, and I hated where she made us live and she was cruel and mean and beastly to us and we ran away. I saw an advertisement in *The Times* about Folly Cottage and I came down and rented it. I pretended to the old lady who owned it that my aunt would be coming too, in case she wouldn't let me have it being so young. And I pretended to Mrs. Trent later that I had an aunt in the background when I came for the job. And the old lady let me have the cottage, and I stole fifty pounds out of my aunt's bag—only it was our money really—and we came here. And I got a job and the children went to school and I was trying to manage until next year when the friends who looked after us in Kenya after Mummy died were coming to England, because I knew they would believe me and help me. And now with your interference have given us away to that horrible woman who is my Aunt Evelyn. I could kill you!"

Susan's head was bent before Belle's blazing and accusing eyes. "Oh help, oh help!" she thought. "What have I done? Oh, why couldn't

I mind my own business? But I only wanted to
help——"

"But listen, Belle," Midge said, "Mrs. Forester
is sweet!"

"Yes!" said Belle bitterly. "That's what *you*
think! That's what the lawyer thought! But
we've lived with her!"

There was the sound of a car stopping in the
lane. "Oh gosh, here she comes!" murmured
Midge.

Mary went over to Belle and took her hand;
Robert, in what Susan would have thought a very
touching way if she had been able to raise her
eyes and see it, went and stood protectingly in
front of his sisters. Mrs. Forester, glowing and
eager, stepped into the room and stood there.
Cousin Barbara and Aunt Lucy and Charlotte and
Bill hovered uncertainly behind her.

"Are you my nieces and nephew?" said Mrs.
Forester.

"That's not my aunt," said Belle in a wondering
voice, "that's not Evelyn Gardiner!"

Mrs. Forester looked at the little group standing
huddled together against the wall, their defiance
changing to bewilderment, and she smiled at
them. "Are you really the children of Anna
Gardiner who married David Smith and lived in
Nakuru?"

"Yes," said Belle, "but you're not Evelyn
Gardiner."

"Well," said Mrs. Forester, "my name is
certainly Evelyn Gardiner—or it was before it
became Evelyn Forester, and I had a sister Anna

who was killed in Kenya two years ago. Where
have you been since your mother died?"

"I don't understand," said Belle, and now she
didn't look so pale or so defiant, she only looked
bewildered. "*Our* Aunt Evelyn met us in London
and we lived with her for two months—she wasn't
what I expected Mummy's sister to be, yet I
recognised her, too, from photos that Mummy
had before—before Daddy made her put them all
away——"

Midge whispered to Susan, "This is a fine way
to clear up a mystery. You've landed us in
another!"

That was true enough, but Susan wasn't caring.
This reunion scene was a little peculiar, she had
to admit, but it didn't seem to be the dreadful
fiasco it had promised to be when Belle had turned
on her, and she was so thankful for small mercies
that she could have shouted for joy. Still, somebody had to clear up this further mystery. "But
Belle, isn't this," she said, indicating Mrs. Forester,
"the horrible aunt you were telling us about?"

"Of course she's not," said Belle. She looked at
the pretty and kind-looking Mrs. Forester and
gave a little shy smile. "If only she were our
aunt," she thought. "Only she could *never* be
horrible!"

"Well then," said Susan, with the air of a
conjurer pulling a rabbit out of a hat, "there are
two Evelyn Gardiners! And which is the right
one?"

"Oh, I am, I'm sure!" said Mrs. Forester.

CHAPTER FOURTEEN

THE MYSTERY SOLVED

EVERYBODY SUDDENLY began talking at once, putting forward their own ideas. The Carmichaels and Susan and Aunt Lucy and Cousin Barbara buzzed excitedly, clamouring for details or supplying them to the best of their ability. Mrs. Forester talked to Belle, asking her questions, which at last Belle seemed willing to answer. Bill told Robert that he jolly well hoped that Mrs. Forester *was* his real aunt because she had a very decent house with a mill-stream going underneath it, and Robert said gosh, he hoped so too! Mary was the only one who said very little. Her previous experience of aunts hadn't been too happy, but this one certainly looked a lot better than the other one, and it would be nice if this turned out to be the right one. She ran upstairs and brought down the photograph of her mother. Mrs. Forester said that she had had the very same photo at home only it had been lost; and Susan begged Belle to show Mrs. Forester the ring that she wore on a chain round her neck with the initials on it. Belle said, with a slight return to her old guarded and suspicious manner, how did Susan know what was on the ring, and Susan blushed and said hurriedly, oh, never mind that now. Mrs. Forester said that there was no doubt that Belle was her niece, but that she thought her name was Evelyn? And Belle said that so it was Evelyn—Evelyn Annabel, but after the family quarrel her father had said that she must be called Annabel in future. When they ran away from Aunt Evelyn, or the person whom they thought was Aunt Evelyn, she had called herself Belle as a sort of disguise—Smith was such a common name that she didn't see much point in changing that—and she had tried to change the children's names too, but it was hopeless, they *never* remembered—and as a matter of fact, she had occasionally forgotten herself that she was Belle; and Susan nudged Charlotte and said, "There you are, didn't I tell you?" And Cousin Barbara, when she could get a hearing, suggested that they should all go back to the farm for tea, which was all ready waiting on the table. They all bundled into the car or on to bicycles, and all through tea the discussion still raged merrily.

"But what I cannot understand," said Mrs. Forester for the twentieth time, "is why I wasn't told about you? And this bogus woman who turned up, how did *she* know about you and who is she?"

And, after all, it was Aunt Lucy who solved *that* mystery, for she suddenly put down the piece of birthday cake that she was in the very act of biting and said dramatically, "Esther Groves!"

Mrs. Forester looked at her vacantly. "What about Esther Groves?"

"Well," said Aunt Lucy, "didn't you tell us that she lived with you and dealt with your correspondence, and then left you very suddenly? She knew all about you and your family, she could easily pass herself off as you before a lawyer, someone who had never met either of you——"

"Oh," cried Mrs. Forester, "and my birth certificate that disappeared! Oh, but I can't believe it of poor Esther Groves!"

"Poor Esther Groves! I never did like her," said Cousin Barbara. She rose there and then, right in the middle of tea and darted off to the drawing-room. She came back with the photograph album and opened it at the twenty-year-old snapshots. "Now," she said, thrusting the album at Belle, "is there anyone there who looks like the person who called herself your Aunt Evelyn?"

"Oh yes," said Belle, or rather Annabel, pointing, "there she is——!"

"You see, Evelyn?" said Cousin Barbara complacently, "Esther Groves!"

"Well, really," said Mrs. Forester, "I just can't take it in. But in any case, Annabel, I'll take you three up with me to see the lawyer to-morrow——"

"Oh," said Annabel, blenching a little, "that lawyer! He wouldn't believe me when I went to him and told him what Aunt—what that woman was doing to us."

"Never mind, honey," said Mrs. Forester rather grimly, "I'll fix that lawyer!"

At last, this most exhilarating party broke up. Mrs. Forester telephoned her husband at his office to prepare him a little for his new family, and

would have carried them off to the Mill-House
there and then. But Annabel and Mary and
Robert suddenly became rather shy—at least,
Annabel could see that Mary and Robert did, so
she said tentatively that perhaps they had better
stay at Folly Cottage that night. "Besides," she
said, "I must pop over here in the morning to do
the chores before we come up to London with
you——"

Cousin Barbara said, "Over my dead body will
you do a stroke of work in this house to-morrow,
Belle!"

And Aunt Lucy said, "I should think not,
indeed. Susan and Midge can do the chores
to-morrow."

"Well, of *course*," said Midge, "only I was rather
hoping for a long lie to-morrow, as I feel
absolutely *dead*. This has been quite a day and
remember that some of us had no sleep last
night."

"I *am* remembering," said Aunt Lucy. "In fact
I think it would be a very good idea if you all
had your baths and went to bed *now*. Or at least
after the tea-things are washed up."

"Well," said Annabel, "at least I can wash the
tea-things. And Mrs. Trent, if you were wanting
some help now that I shan't be here, there was
a rather pathetic little maid in that terrible
boarding-house, I'm sure the country would do
her good. Of course, she might not suit you and
she might not want to come, but I should like
to help her if I could because she tried to be kind
to us."

"I'll look into it," said Cousin Barbara. "But I'll never get a worker like you, Belle!"

"I'll help wash up," said Susan.

It was scarcely possible, Susan thought, that the morose, rather sullen Belle should in such a short time become the bright, almost sparkling Annabel. She positively *chattered*, Susan thought, as they did the dishes.

"I should think," said Annabel, "that Mrs. Forester, or rather Aunt Evelyn, only I'll *never* get used to calling her that, after the other terrible woman, would be a nice sort of aunt, shouldn't you? You know her better than I do, although it seems ridiculous that you should."

"Oh, goodness yes!" said Susan. "Mrs. Forester is a darling."

"And Susan," said Annabel, suddenly very busy in the sink, "if it hadn't been for you we should never have found her——"

"Ugh away, you would so," said Susan gruffly, much moved. "Whenever Mrs. Forester saw that lawyer it would all have been cleared up."

"But she might never have found us!" cried Annabel. "I was thinking of moving the children again only not knowing where to go. You did it all and I'm terribly sorry I spoke to you the way I did."

"Ugh, I deserved every word," said Susan in a sudden burst of humility. "It turned out all right this time, but really I'd be better minding my own business. Supposing I'd handed you over to the bad auntie!"

"Yes, but you didn't," said Annabel. "If I'd had any sense, I'd have gone to Mrs. Trent and told her the whole thing when first I heard Evelyn Gardiner's name. I should have known that Mrs. Trent would see that we were all right. But I was too scared."

"Oh help, I should think so!" said Susan, shuddering as she remembered what Annabel had told them of the bogus Aunt Evelyn. "And I hope," she added viciously, "that Mrs. Forester does fix that lawyer to-morrow!"

Early next morning, Mrs. Forester collected Annabel and Mary and Robert at Folly Cottage, and everyone gave them a rousing cheer as they passed on their way to London.

Susan and the Carmichaels prepared to spend a quiet and dull morning after the terrific excitements of the day before, but it was unexpectedly enlivened by a visit from Mr. Bristow.

He arrived on his bicycle in his somewhat ponderous way. Cousin Barbara offered him a cup of tea, which he said he would appreciate very much, and they all sat in the kitchen drinking tea or cocoa according to their taste.

"This will be quite a feather in your cap, Mr. Bristow," said Cousin Barbara, "capturing the Mad Collector!"

"You're right, Mrs. Trent, mum," said Mr. Bristow. "Sarge is that jealous he's been pea-green ever since I brought it off—with the help of the young ladies and gentleman here. But I've got a little surprise for you. I reckon you've all been thinking that that there Smith was the Mad Collector?"

"Well, of course!"

"We captured him for you, didn't we?"

"Who else *could* be?"

"Oh, Mr. Bristow, *don't* say there has been a mistake after all!"

Constable Bristow was sitting back in his chair, beaming and enjoying the sensation he had caused. "No, no," he said, "we've got the Collector all right, all right, but he's not the little old joker we thought——"

"Mr. Bristow," Charlotte interrupted in an awed voice, "you're not trying to tell us that the Mad Collector is Miss Frame!"

Babel again broke out.

"She *couldn't* be!"

"*Not* the Dresden shepherdess!"

"That dainty little creature!"

"Mr. Bristow, how did you find out? Did Mr. Smith give her away?"

"No," said Mr. Bristow, when they were ready to listen to him, "give him credit, he wouldn't say one word against her. No, she made a statement. She had some hold over him, she didn't say what it was, and she made him help her with her schemes, doing the framing and that, but *she* did the actual robberies! The only robbery, or attempted robbery he did was when he came here to get the map back and he was so scared that he brought the gun, which was an old service revolver, the silly young man, only it wasn't loaded——"

"But if Miss Frame was the Mad Collector," interrupted Susan, ignoring the bit about the gun because it made her feel very silly, "why did she let us have the wrong map in the first place? And once we had got the map with the Letter behind it and she came for it and saw the frames had been changed, why didn't she do something?"

"We could have changed the frames without finding the letter," said Midge. "And what could she do without giving herself away?"

"Besides, she did do something," said Bill, "she sent her cat's paw that night!"

"I suppose she thought it was too risky, robbing a house where the people knew her so well," said Charlotte. "Although I must say, I can't visualise her doing any robberies."

"She was smart enough at the robberies," said Mr. Bristow. "She used to get into those big houses where there were valuable old manuscripts and things like that on the pretext of looking at their bits of old china and stuff, and while she was there she'd note where the valuables were, and how many of a staff there were, and if there were any dogs in the house and how the windows were fastened and useful little bits of information like that—she was a sharp one, was Miss Frame, going about the countryside on her bicycle!"

"Well, when she was as smart as all that, if you can call that sort of thing smart," said Midge, "it's a wonder that she was so silly as to give us the map with the Folding Letter in it. She made a big mistake there."

"Ah, I reckon that was Smith's mistake, not

her's, he was supposed to keep the prepared maps in the cellar," said Constable Bristow. "There was another man in it too, he used to come down to the little antique shop and 'buy' the maps and take them to America and sell the valuable old manuscripts—Miss Frame has a very nice pile of dollars in a bank in New York——"

"The creature!" said Charlotte.

Constable Bristow finally talked himself off.

"I jolly well hope he gets promoted for this," said Bill.

"And I'll tell you another thing," said Susan, "I jolly well think he ought to get share of our reward when we get it——"

"Carried *nem* absolutely *con*," said Midge.

At twelve o'clock Mrs. Forester telephoned. "My dear," she said to Cousin Barbara, "I've got that lawyer *grovelling*—I'll tell you all about it when we get home. We're going to do a little shopping and have lunch in town with their new uncle—I'm so thrilled with my family that I can hardly speak, but we'll call in and see you on our way home and give you all the news——"

The shopping had consisted of a bicycle each for Annabel, Mary and Robert, which were to be sent down by rail, and some new clothes. Another day was to be devoted to choosing new wallpapers and curtains for their rooms in the Mill-House. Apart altogether from the question of clothes and bicycles, Annabel and the children had already completely succumbed to the charm of Mrs. Forester—it was almost like finding again a younger, gayer mother. Annabel, in her conscientious way, couldn't help worrying a little about how Mr. Forester—or Uncle James, as she was beginning to call him, a little awkwardly, was going to react to a houseful of children, although she had to admit that he had been perfectly sweet at lunch and had given them salmon and pêche melba.

"Oh, and *Susan*, if you could have seen that lawyers' face when we all marched in! Of course he had already had quite a shock when Aunt Evelyn's lawyers had got in touch with him and had been frantically trying to trace That Woman——"

"Why, yes," interrupted Mrs. Forester, "I should think so indeed, because she has managed to get away with eight thousand pounds of the children's money!"

"Oh, let her have the money!" cried Annabel. "What does the money matter? We've got rid of her and we've found *you*. It's worth it."

Susan gazed at her, dewy-eyed and beaming at the whole romantic situation. "All the same," she said, her Scottish blood rising, "that's all very well, but I don't see why that horrible woman should have eight thousand pounds of your money. How did she manage it?"

"Well," said Mrs. Forester, "it was as we had guessed, I think. The lawyers wrote to Miss Evelyn Gardiner—I got married, remember, after the quarrel with my brother-in-law—saying that my sister had been killed and had left her money to me in trust for the children. Esther Groves opened the letter, and saw a chance of getting something for herself out of it by passing herself off as me. With the papers she stole from me—because I'm sure now that that is what she did—she claimed to be Evelyn Gardiner, and on the pretext of buying a house and furniture and so on for the children managed to get about eight thousand pounds into her clutches——"

"She certainly didn't spend a penny on us," said Annabel. "She made us live in that awful cheap boarding-house——"

"She wouldn't even buy us warm clothes at first," said Mary. "I was cold all the time."

"Well, darlings," said Mrs. Forester, "forget about all that dreadful time—now you shall have all the clothes you need—and toys and things of course. Oh, and schools—we must see about schools."

Charlotte said, "Couldn't Annabel come to St. Ronan's with us? Mary and Robert are rather young for boarding-school—and actually Annabel is rather old, but as the daughter of one old girl and the niece of another, surely they'd let her in?"

"I suppose that you do want to go back to school, Annabel?" Mrs. Forester said. "You needn't, you know."

"Well, I think I'd like to, Aunt Evelyn," said Annabel, "because I should like to go to the university."

"Then I'll go and see the headmistress as soon as possible," said Mrs. Forester.

Midge and Susan thought it was rather eccentric of Annabel to *want* to go back to school when she had a perfectly good chance of giving it up for ever, but if she *had* to go to school, they thought, she certainly couldn't do better than St. Ronan's.

"I expect that you'll be in a much higher form than us, Annabel," said Susan, "even although you've missed so much, but I'll be glad to help you to get into the way of things, for I'm not much more than a new girl myself and I know the snags——"

"Oh golly," muttered Charlotte, "if Susan's going to give you a helping hand, Annabel, watch out!"

Annabel said vehemently, "Well, if it *hadn't* been for Susan's helping hand, remember, Mary and Robert and I shouldn't be here with a new aunt and uncle and a home and, and *everything*!"

"Goodness, neither you would," said Midge. She and Charlotte looked at each other apprehensively. "Oh dear," said Midge, "now there's going to be no holding her!"

THE END